# Don't Worry About Me.
# I'll Be All Right.

# Don't Worry About Me.
# Me.
# I'll Be All Right.

By Brannon Kirk O'Neal

ISBN: 978-0-578-55610-9

# Chapter 1

I have always hated the name Maggie. It sounds like the name of an old lady who knits. I do not knit, and I am not old, but I am named Maggie. My mother said the name comes from Maggie Millburn, who was the woman who first discovered the Durmon virus.

*What a silly name for a virus,* is all I can think.

This story is not really about the Durmon virus. This story is mostly about a boy named Paul, a girl named Paula, and me.

Paul was a boy who used to live on my street. Back then there were tons of people, and the streets were crowded with smelly cars. I like the streets much better now, but it is certainly a shame how they got to be this way.

Paul and I hung out a lot back then, because he was the only other kid on the street, and I wanted another kid to hang out with. I couldn't bear to talk to adults. All they ever wanted to know was how old I was and how I was doing in school. My conversations with Paul were far more interesting.

Paul read books all the time in order to be smart. His father had told him that the smartest people were the people who read a lot of books.

Personally I think that Paul's father was the stupidest person of all time, and he didn't know anything at all. That's probably why what happened to him, happened to him.

This story starts with the summer that it was so hot, because during that summer is when everything happened.

It was so hot that summer that you couldn't breathe practically. If you walked outside, it was as if you'd walked into an oven. It was the summer that Paul got his first letter from Paula. It was also the summer that I got my pink bike. I was riding that bike everywhere I went that summer.

At the start of that summer, the Durmon virus was dormant, the people on the radio said. According to my mother, it had been dormant since the day it was discovered, and it would stay that way forever. Boy was she wrong about that.

Paul was a really nice boy. He was quiet. He had very smooth black hair, which he combed with a little black comb. I liked to watch Paul comb his hair. He always looked so calm when he combed his hair.

I have black hair too, but mine is not smooth like Paul's. Mother told me once that my hair is called Afro-textured.

\*\*\*

On the day that I got my pink bike, I rode it to Paul's house to show him. I fell down three times and cut my knee the third time. Blood slid down my leg after that, and it felt warm and slippery. I walked my bike the rest of the way, because I didn't want to get blood on it.

When I got to Paul's house, he was sitting in the rocking chair on the porch, reading. The book he was reading was called *The Flight of the Nightingale*, by Cassandra Pop. I don't read that book until later on.

"Hello, Paul," I said, when I saw him there.

"Hello to you," he said, without looking at me.

I stood and looked at Paul and held my bike up, because I didn't want it to get dirty. Paul kept reading. He was finishing his chapter. He always did that when I came by. Once his chapter was over, we could play pirates, or poke sticks in the dirt and look for bugs, or look at the encyclopedia.

Paul's father owned an entire set of encyclopedias, which were really big books with information and sometimes pictures in them too. They were great books to look at while lying on your belly with the book set out in front of you. That was how Paul and I read them. I liked to look at one encyclopedia very much because there was a picture in it of a statue of a man, but the man did not have any clothes on. When Paul saw me looking at the picture, he told me not to. I thought the picture was interesting, that was all.

\*\*\*

When Paul finished his chapter, he put a bookmark in his place and closed the book. Paul's bookmark had a Bible verse written on it. The verse said, "I can do all things through Christ which strengtheneth me." Paul always used that bookmark, which was a gift from his aunt.

I do not understand why someone would give a bookmark as a gift. A book would be a better gift than a bookmark. After all, a bookmark is no good without a book to put it in.

"Well," said Paul, standing up and putting the book on the rocking chair. "Have you got something to show me?"

Paul came down the steps of his porch and walked up to my bike. He put his hands on his hips and looked at it. He was wearing a pair of blue shorts and a white shirt that day. With his hands on his hips, he looked very serious.

"It's a neat bike," he told me.

"Do you like it, really?" I asked him.

"It's very pink," he said, putting his finger on his chin. "I do not like that part, but it looks swell, besides."

"How could you not like the pink part?" I asked him. "The pink part is the best part."

"Really?" said Paul, looking at it again.

I held the bike out and shook the handlebars so that he would see how fine it looked, pink and all.

"Your leg is bleeding," said Paul.

I looked down and so it was. The blood had gone down and stained my sandal. There were drops of blood on the sidewalk too.

"It doesn't hurt," I told him, and that's the truth. It didn't hurt at all. I couldn't even feel it.

"It doesn't hurt at all?" asked Paul, kneeling to get a better look at the cut.

"Nope," I said. "It just feels a bit slimy, is all."

"Can I touch it?" Paul asked.

"If you want to," I said to him.

Paul put his finger on my cut and suddenly it started to hurt really bad. I did not mean to, but I began to cry. I really did not mean to do that. Paul ran into his house and got his mother, and she put a Band-Aid on the spot. The Band-Aid took the pain away right away, and I was able to stop crying, which was a real relief.

I hate to cry. I hate it so much that I don't even do it anymore. I've managed to stop crying completely. No matter how sad I get, I do not cry. These days I don't even need to cry. I do a lot of silly things now, so that I don't feel sad or like crying. Even if I do feel like crying, I do not do it. I think that people cry because there is an open bottle behind their eyes that pours water out when they get sad or hurt. In order to stop crying, all you have to do is put a cap on the bottle.

# Chapter 2

Paul's house was the biggest on the street. It had two floors, a basement, and an attic. The attic was a marvelous little room with a round window in it that could be looked out of. I often saw Paul's head looking out of that window when I went by. He liked his attic very much.

Paul and I spent a lot of time together in his attic. The attic had the most marvelous things in it. There were loads of costumes up there, and we would dress up in them and put on plays. Our best play was one Paul thought of, where we were both pirates.

My pirate costume was a large green hat with a feather on it and a fluffy scarf. Paul's pirate costume was a long white shirt, a red vest, and a pair of boots that were too big and made thumping noises when he walked in them. The play always started with one of us boarding the other's ship for a battle, because having a battle was the most fun.

"Get off my ship," was what we said if someone came onto our ship.

Can you imagine being a real pirate? I think it would be just great. I love treasure and jewels, and I think that's what pirates love too.

After I had gotten better at riding my bike without falling down, I rode it to Paul's house, and up we went to the attic to play pirates.

"Get off my ship," Paul said to me when I climbed over the boxes that separated our ships.

"I won't," I said.

"Oh, come on," said Paul, "just do it. I'm not ready for an attack just yet."

"All right," I said.

I climbed back over the boxes to my boat.

"Let me know when you're ready for an attack, and I'll come back."

"Just you wait," said Paul.

Paul was working on the buttons on his pirate costume. He always had to make sure his buttons were perfect.

"Are you ready yet?" I asked him.

"Do you know," said Paul, "that there are volcanoes at the bottom of the ocean?"

Paul was always telling me things like this. He must have known everything there was in the whole world.

"Are there really?" I asked him.

"Yes," said Paul, "and they make the water so hot that it would kill a human."

"Why doesn't the water cool off the volcano?" I asked.

"Because volcanoes are too hot for that," said Paul.

"How hot are volcanoes?" I asked.

"About one million degrees," said Paul.

Paul was always right about these things, so I had to believe him, even though I didn't.

*** 

I think maybe I will go to the ocean and swim to the bottom and look for volcanoes. I think that is a good thing to do.

*** 

"Can I tell you a secret?" Paul asked me.

"No," I said.

I do not like secrets. I think secrets are nasty. My mother said that if anyone ever told me a secret, I should go straight to her and tell her what the secret was. I always told her whenever I heard a secret.

"What if it isn't really a secret?" asked Paul, peeking at me over the boxes that separated our ships. "What if it's just something that I want to tell you?"

"OK, then tell me," I said.

Paul climbed over the boxes to my ship, and so I said, "Get off my ship."

"I'm not playing pirates right now," said Paul.

But it was too late. I had already drawn my sword, which was a broken lamp with no lampshade on it. I stabbed Paul in the gut and told him that he was dead, which was true. He was dead because I had stabbed him.

"I'm really not playing right now," said Paul, but he was because he was dressed as a pirate, and he was on my boat. "Look," said Paul, holding up an envelope that was a yellowish color. It looked as if it would taste like vanilla.

"Is that what I think it is?" I asked.

"Yes," said Paul.

Up to that point, I had never heard of a child getting a letter. Letters were things adults got in the mail. Letters were not for children.

What Paul held in his hand was a letter. It was addressed to him, which was incredibly strange.

"Did you open it?" I asked.

"Not yet," said Paul. "I am frightened. What if I am being sent to military school?"

Paul had once read a book that was all about military school. The book described military school as a place where bad boys went when they had tormented their parents too much. The book was about a boy named Abraham who had been sent to the military school by accident. Abraham was forced to eat oatmeal for breakfast, do pushups for lunch, and only bathe once a week. Later in the book, Abraham escaped and ran back home where his mother and father wept and hugged him and fed him pancakes for three days straight. It was one of Paul's favorite books because he liked to read stories where bad things happened to good people.

There is something nice about stories where bad things happen to good people. I think this is because everyone believes they are a good person, and so when something bad happens to them, they feel like the character in the book. When they remember how the book ends, they think, *Well, things are bad now, but in the end, I'll get hugs and lots of pancakes.*

The reason Paul thought he was going to be sent to military school was because his father was always mad at him about something. If Paul left his toys in the living room, his father would yell, "My son is a pig who leaves messes everywhere." If Paul did not finish his food, his father would yell, "My son is an ingrate who doesn't care that children in other countries are starving." If Paul was ever lazy, talked back, or did anything disobedient, he was punished cruelly. He would be sent to bed without dinner, spanked, or pinched in the ear. Paul believed his father wanted to send him to military school any minute.

"What should I do?" Paul asked.

"You should open it," I said. "If it is the military, we will burn the letter, so no one will ever find it, and then you won't have to go."

Paul tore open the envelope and pulled out a letter written in really neat handwriting.

*Dear Paul,*

*My name is Paula. I am writing you this letter because I wanted to say hello to you. My mother is teaching me how to send letters, because she says it is an important skill. I don't know a thing to say.*

*I am very tall for my age, and I have red hair. I read a lot of books, because there are no children where I live besides me. My mother says she knows your mother from a long time ago. She says you are a nice boy. I am very frightened to write a letter to someone, so I hope you are nice.*

*My favorite book is a book called* The Very Dark Woods, *because it is spooky, and I like spooky things, and because it is sad, and I like sad things too. I would like to know what you think.*

*Also, I like a song called "Good Night," because it is very beautiful.*

*Yours truly,*

*Paula.*

"Wow," said Paul when he was done reading.

# Chapter 3

Paul was so fascinated by the letter that he read it several times. He was thrilled with the letter. It was a letter just for him. It was his letter. I was extremely jealous. I didn't know until then, but I had always wanted a letter all for myself.

Paul was very eager to read the book Paula had said she liked so much. He made his mother take him to the library that same day, so he could get it.

When he got back from the library, which is a very boring place, because it is so quiet there, he read for the rest of the night and did not stop once, unless it was to read his letter again. There was nothing for me to do at Paul's house but go home, and so I did. But Paul kept on reading.

\*\*\*

In the morning I woke up sweating because it was so hot. I ate breakfast, which was cereal in a bowl with milk on it, and I went back to Paul's house because I could not believe that he had really gotten a letter. I needed to see it for myself again.

When I got to Paul's house, I found out he was not allowed out of his room because he had been reading after he was supposed to go to sleep. His father had seen the light on under the door and made a real fuss. I could just hear his nasty voice.

"Please," I said to Paul's mother, who was very quiet and nice, "I really must speak to Paul. I have been thinking of things to say to him all morning, and if I don't say them, I will surely forget them."

Paul's mother patted me on the head, which made me feel short, and told me that I could go on into his room if I kept it a secret. Well, the first thing I did when I got home was tell my mother that I had been in Paul's room and that it was supposed to be a secret.

"What did you do with Paul in his room?" she asked me.

"We talked about a book," I told her. And that's the truth too.

When I went into Paul's room, he had finished the book that Paula had talked about. It was sitting on his bed next to his pillow.

The book was a hardcover, and it had that clear plastic wrapping on it that all libraries put on their books to keep them from getting ruined. The front cover had a drawing of a black forest on it, with snow on the ground. In swirly letters at the bottom were the words "*The Very Dark Woods*, by Jasmine Line."

"Did you read Paula's book?" I asked.

"I did," said Paul.

"Was it very interesting and good?" I asked.

"It was one of the greatest books I have ever read," said Paul.

This is the story of *The Very Dark Woods*, according to Paul: Once there was an old woman who lived in a small cottage next to some woods. She was really super old and wrinkled and limped when she walked.

One day this old woman heard the most beautiful music coming from inside the forest. The woman was confused because she lived far away from civilization, so how could there be music? She walked to the edge of the forest and tried to look inside, but all she could see was darkness because of how dark the woods were.

She decided to walk into the forest a little bit to see if she could find the music, so she got a lantern and started walking. Well, as she walked further into the woods, it got darker and darker, but the woman also noticed that she was getting younger and younger. She went from being an old woman to a middle-aged woman, and from a middle-aged woman to a young woman, and from a young woman to a teenager, and from a teenager to a little girl. As she transformed, her limping stopped, and she started to feel good, because she wasn't old anymore. Well, when she was finally transformed into a little girl, she came upon a very old, very tall tree with a hole in it. The music was coming from inside the hole.

The little girl, who had been an old woman at the start of the book, went into the hole and crawled her way to a room where a merry party was being held with many small animals. There were squirrels, rabbits, robins, and woodpeckers. The creatures were happy to meet the little girl, and they fed her lots of food from their table. She became so full after a while that she fell asleep.

When the little girl awoke, she was locked in a small cell inside a horrible dungeon. The dungeon was part of an evil castle at the center of the woods. The castle belonged to an evil creature called a Gnagdall. The Gnagdall was definitely evil and horrifying to look at too. It kept itself alive by making things suffer. The girl had ended up in the Gnagdall's castle because the little animals had given her to the Gnagdall while she was asleep, so their own lives would be spared. It was a selfish and nasty thing to do.

While the girl was at the castle, she was forced to do chores like cleaning and scrubbing. She was very unhappy about this, and she wanted to go home.

As she explored the castle, which was very large and very evil, she met other unfortunate people and animals who had been captured. She met another little girl, and the two of them made a plan to kill the Gnagdall and set everyone free.

They snuck into the Gnagdall's chambers while it slept one night. They had to be careful not to look at it, because if they did, they would surely scream and give themselves away. They carefully lifted a large sword, which belonged to the Gnagdall, and they thrust the sword into the Gnagdall's chest. The Gnagdall awoke and let out a painful screech. It staggered around and gurgled while the girls screamed, and suddenly it fell over dead. The castle melted away and everyone was free.

The young girl was so happy to be free, but she noticed that she and all the people she had set free were starting to grow old again. She turned and ran, but she didn't know where she was going because she was so far in the forest. She wandered aimlessly around the woods growing older, and older, and older. She asked many of the animals if they knew the way out, but none of them did. Finally she could not walk anymore because she was too tired. She sat down on a log, an old wrinkled woman with sore feet, and began to cry.

As she cried a blue bird with a long beak and long legs came out of the darkness. "Why are you crying?" asked the blue bird.

"I am crying because I will die in this forest," said the old woman, who had been a young girl.

"Would you like a wish?" said the blue bird. "I am a bird who gives wishes to people and then grants them whenever they like."

"I would like a wish," said the old woman.

"You have one, then," said the blue bird. "I give everybody one wish. Be sure to use it wisely."

"I wish," said the old woman, "that I never came into this evil forest."

The second the old woman said that she was suddenly back in her house at the edge of the forest with no memory of the Gnagdall or anything. She was happy to be at her house. She didn't even know she had ever left it.

Suddenly she heard music coming from the forest. "I wonder what that could be," she said.

And that was how the story ended.

Paul said there were two morals in the story. The first moral was to not trust strangers, no matter how nice they seemed, and the second moral was to be careful what you wished for.

I think that if I could wish for anything, it would be that the Durmon virus never existed.

# Chapter 4

Paul was very eager to write a letter back to Paula. When I visited him next, I found him in the attic with a piece of paper and a pencil. He was lying on his stomach with the paper in front of him and the eraser of the pencil up his nose. He looked very smart lying there like that. He was trying to think of things to say.

What he had written was this:

*Dear Paula,*

*It is me, Paul. I read* The Very Dark Woods, *and I thought it was good. I liked it a lot. I read as many books as I can, because I am trying to become as smart as possible.*

*Do you know a lot about volcanoes? I like volcanoes because there are some that are underwater. Lava is very hot, so it is interesting that it is underwater. Don't you think so?*

*I was very pleased to get a letter from you because I have never received a letter before.*

That was all that he had written. That and no more.

"What are you doing?" was the first thing I asked Paul when I saw him.

"I'm writing a letter to Paula," he said. "That is what people do when they receive letters from people. It is not easy."

"Do you want to play pirates?" I asked, because that was what I wanted to do.

Paul did not want to play pirates that day, because he wanted to write a letter to Paula. He asked me what I thought the letter should say, and I suggested that he tell Paula about our pirates play. Paul did not want to tell Paula about that, because he was afraid that she would think it was stupid.

*What's so bad about being stupid?* is all I can wonder.

I left Paul in the attic and went to the kitchen for some ice cream or something.

This was how I got ice cream at Paul's house: You see, my mother always told me not to ask for sweets when I was at someone else's house, because it was rude, so I always had to ask in a way where it didn't seem like I was really asking.

"Hello, ma'am," I said to Paul's mother, "it sure is hot outside, isn't it?"

"Yes," said Paul's mother, who was cleaning the table with a washcloth.

"It's very possible to get dehydrated in hot air like this, isn't it ma'am?" I asked.

"I suppose if you weren't careful," said Paul's mother without even looking at me.

"I sure would hate to get dehydrated and die in the heat, wouldn't you, ma'am?" I asked.

"Oh I think so," she said.

"Yeah," I said, "that's why people on the radio say, 'be sure to eat lots of ice cream.' Do you listen to the radio, ma'am?"

Paul's mother finally stopped what she was doing and looked at me. "Well," she said, "do you know what? I think you could use some hydrating like the people on the radio say. What do you think?"

Now this was the trickiest part about getting ice cream from Paul's mother, because my mother always said that if I was offered something at someone else's house, it was only to be polite, and so I should say no out of politeness as well.

"Oh, ma'am," I said to Paul's mother, trying my hardest to look dehydrated and miserable. "I'm all right. I don't need any ice cream or anything."

Of course, Paul's mother gave me an entire scoop of ice cream after that. She let me sit at the table and eat it while she went around cleaning.

Paul's mother liked to clean things very much, it seemed like. She washed the dishes and then the floors, the windows, the carpets, the cabinets, the tabletops, and so on. It never seemed to end. I was very careful to not make a mess of my ice cream because I didn't want to make any more messes for her to have to clean up.

I managed to eat the whole bowl of ice cream without trouble, but when I tried to pour the last of it into my mouth, I spilled a big drop of melted ice cream on the floor. I was horrified; you can imagine. Just as I noticed the drop, Paul's mother came in. Frantically I put my foot on top of the drop so she wouldn't see it.

"All finished?" she asked me, looking in my bowl.

"Yes," I barely whispered.

She took the bowl and the spoon and put them in the sink and began to wash them.

I lifted my foot enough to look under it and, sure enough, there was still a drop of ice cream there. In fact, putting my foot on it had smeared the ice cream into an even bigger spot. When Paul's mother turned around to look at me, I slammed my foot onto the spot again. I really didn't know what to do. I wanted to run away and never come back, and never see Paul's mother again. I wished Paul would come down from the attic and ask for a bowl of ice cream for himself, so I could blame the spot on him. I imagined it in my head. I would scream, "Paul, you've spilled a drop on the floor!" and I would point at the spot. Paul would feel terrible about spilling, and so I would say, "Never mind, it could happen to anyone." And that would cheer him up. I was very good at cheering Paul up.

Now I realize how silly it all was.

I was so terrified of Paul's mother seeing the mess I had made, because I was embarrassed about it. Really though, it didn't matter that much. It was just a mess that would have to be cleaned up. That's all that messes are: things that have to be cleaned up.

What I did about that mess under my shoe was this: I sat in that chair with my foot over the spot until Paul's mom left the kitchen to clean the bathroom. Once she was gone, I ran out of the house and climbed onto my bike and rode home as fast as I could.

My mother asked me why I was all sweaty when I got home. The answer was because I had pedaled my bike so fast even though it was so hot. I really was hot when I got home, and so I drank a glass of water.

My mother could tell that I was bothered by something, but she couldn't figure out what it was. The thing that I was bothered about was the mess that I had left on Paul's mother's floor. I was sad because I knew I should have told her I had spilled, but for some reason, I didn't. I don't know why. I just couldn't.

I didn't have too much of an appetite that night, and so I didn't eat too much.

I kept thinking about the spot. When Paul's mother found that spot on her floor, she would definitely know it was from me. That's what was driving me crazy. She probably saw it and thought, *Maggie is the type of girl who makes a mess and then just leaves it for someone else to clean up. How inconsiderate.* I don't think I'm inconsiderate. I just don't think sometimes, that's all.

That night when I was trying to go to sleep, I just couldn't. I kept thinking about how I had left the drop on the floor. I felt so guilty that I just had to kick my feet every five minutes and roll over and let out a huff of breath. I was scared to go back to Paul's house and see his mother again. I was scared she would ask me about the spot. She never did.

# Chapter 5

Despite being a small boy, Paul was very brave. He would stand up to the meanest and nastiest bullies when we were at school. I don't know why he did that. I really don't know why he did that.

I was always glad when I saw Paul being brave, because I felt like as long as he was being brave, I didn't have to be. I could be just as scared as I wanted to.

Of course, now I can't do that. Now I have to be brave all by myself. The first time I really had to be brave all by myself was when Mother didn't come home anymore.

When it was summertime, Paul was happiest because he didn't have to go to school and be brave there. In the summer he could stay at home with his mother, and with me if I visited him. You don't have to be very brave to do that.

\*\*\*

This is the bravest thing I ever saw Paul do: We were sitting in Paul's backyard, which had a large fence around it. We weren't doing anything, really. We were just lazing around.

Paul was combing his hair with his little black comb, and I was watching him.

I think combs are so fascinating. I wish that everything could be combed. I would comb grass and sand and trees and sidewalks and clothes and water and everything else if I could.

As I watched Paul comb his hair, I sat on the lawn and tugged at blades of grass. I twirled them in my fingers. It was a fine way to spend a day. Suddenly I felt something tickling my foot. I looked, and I got so scared because there was a snake, a real snake, on my foot. The snake licked my toe with its nasty tongue, and I nearly screamed I was so upset.

"Paul," I whispered, so I wouldn't alarm the snake. "There is a snake on my foot."

Paul stopped combing his hair, stood up, and walked over to me. He looked at the snake and told me not to move an inch. While I wasn't moving an inch, Paul reached down and grabbed the snake by the head. He picked the snake up and ran as fast as his small legs would carry him, to the edge of the fence. He chucked the snake over the fence, and the two of us ran inside screaming at the top of our lungs. We were so upset by that snake.

Inside, Paul's mother gave each of us a glass of water with a straw in to make us feel better.

"Do you think it was poisonous?" I asked Paul.

Paul was deathly pale. He looked so frightened with a straw in his mouth.

"I think so," he said. "I think it was poisonous. It looked very poisonous. Didn't you see the spots on it?"

It was true. The snake had spots on it. They were the most poisonous-looking spots I had ever seen.

"Paul," I said very seriously, "you saved my life."

"Did I really?" said Paul.

"I'm sure you did," I told him.

"Wow," said Paul.

That is exactly the kind of thing Paul would say after saving someone's life. He would say "wow" as if he was surprised that he had done such a thing. I think that is what real bravery is. Real bravery is the kind of bravery that surprises the person who does it and makes them say, "I did that?" I am trying to be brave like that now.

*\*\**

When the announcement came out on the radio that the Durmon virus was no longer dormant but had started to attack the cells of all the humans, that was another time when Paul was very brave.

Paul looked at me as the man radio spoke and said, "It'll be all right for us, Maggie. We'll be all right for sure."

I wish Paul were here to say that to me now.

***

But before the radio announced the attack of the Durmon virus, Paul received a second letter from Paula. This letter was written on pink paper, which I did not like because I knew that Paul did not like the color pink. It was, after all, the one thing he had criticized about my pink bike.

"What a shame," I said when Paul opened the letter in the attic, "she used pink paper."

Paul looked at the paper and raised one of his eyebrows.

"I don't mind it so much on paper," Paul said at last.

Well, that made me so angry that I wanted to take the letter and rip it to shreds right in front of him before he had a chance to read it. That would serve him right. I did not like Paula, and I did not like the way Paul just talked and talked about her.

"She has written me a longer letter this time," he said. "I am very excited to read it."

"Would you like it if I wrote you a letter, Paul?" I asked him.

"No," said Paul after thinking and raising his eyebrow again. "You live right down the street, after all. It wouldn't make sense. You could just come and tell me what it was you wanted to say."

At first I went and looked out the window because I didn't want to see the letter or see what it said, but then I decided that I just had to know what it said, and so I went to Paul and looked at it over his shoulder.

*Dear Paul,*

*It is me, Paula, writing another letter to you. I am very surprised and very happy that you read* The Very Dark Woods. *I would like it if you would tell me your favorite book so that I can read it and tell you what I think. Can you do that?*

*I do not know much about volcanoes, but I think they are interesting. Maybe I will become a scientist and study volcanoes when I grow up. I think I would like to be a scientist. I want to study things and make discoveries. I am always trying to discover things, even now. Everywhere I go I am always looking for something to discover.*

*My mother tells me that it has been very hot where you live. Well, it has been very hot here too, but we live in the desert and so it is always hot. You may be surprised to hear this, but I have only seen snow in pictures. I have never had the chance to stand in it and feel it. My mother has, and she says it is quite cold. She says snow is just like ice. I cannot even begin to imagine it. It is very exciting to think about. Perhaps I will become a scientist who studies snow.*

*Do you think you will become a scientist when you grow up? Scientists have to be very smart in order to make discoveries, and they have to read a lot too. I think you would be a perfect scientist, and perhaps we could make discoveries together. I would like that.*

*There are so many things I want to learn about, like electricity and big math equations.*

*Sometimes I wish that I could be an adult already. I am tired of being a child.*

*I wish I could put on a coat, and a pair of neat gloves, and say, "I am a scientist," and go out into the world to make discoveries.*

*That is all for now,*

*Please tell me what your favorite book is and do not forget.*

*Love,*

*Paula.*

*Love?* was all I could think. *Love?*

# Chapter 6

You are probably wondering where my father was for all this time. He did not live with Mother and I. That much is true.

My father left when I was very young, but I was old enough to remember his face. He had a big chin, large brown eyes, and short hair. He was very muscular and, when he gave you a hug, he did not feel soft at all.

My father really did love my mother, and he loved me too. He loved us both very much and did not want to leave us alone. He couldn't stand the thought of leaving us alone.

The reason my father left was to build homes for poor people in another country. My father had a big heart, which made him care about a lot of things. One of the things he cared about were the poor people in another country. My father had once been poor, and he had once lived without a home, and so it made him sad to hear that there were people without homes in other countries. He was the type of person who would think, *How can I feel comfortable in my home, knowing that there is someone else out there who doesn't have one?*

One of the last things my father said to me was, "Be quiet and eat your green beans." It was not the last thing he said to me, but it was one of the last things. I cannot remember what the very last thing he said to me was, but I know it was a nice thing. I wish I could remember it, but my silly brain just can't, no matter how hard I try.

My mother said that my father was a very good singer. She said that when she met him, he was singing a tune that he had made up all by himself. It was his own original song about a pretty girl and a handsome man falling in love. I like songs like that.

Sometimes, when I had been very obedient all day, my mother would tell me a story about my father before I went to sleep.

This is that story: One day my father was getting off a train at a train station. He was on his way home from building automobiles, which was his job at the time. He had not met my mother yet, but he was about to.

As he stepped onto the platform at the train station, he quietly sang the song he wrote. He was singing it to himself. My mother noticed him singing and listened because she loved to listen to people sing. She thought people had the most wonderful singing voices.

When my father saw my mother for the first time, he fell so deeply in love with her that he became dizzy and fell over. My mother laughed when she saw him fall because he looked so silly. She tried to hide her laughter when she saw that he was looking at her, but trying to hide it only made it funnier, and so she laughed harder still. My father could have been embarrassed and mad at my mother for laughing at him, but instead, he smiled widely and laughed along.

He had a very loud, happy laugh. When he laughed, everyone around him was put at ease. When he laughed at what you said, you felt as if you had told the funniest joke in the whole world.

When my father got up from falling over, he walked straight up to my mother and asked her to please have dinner with him. My mother was not hungry, but she said yes anyway because she wanted to stay with my father. She had fallen in love with him at first sight too.

*** 

At dinner that night, my father told my mother about building automobiles, and she told him about serving food to hungry people because my mother was a waitress. My father and my mother got along splendidly. They ended up talking for five hours straight, and they never once ran out of things to talk about in all that time.

At the end of dinner, my father asked for my mother's phone number so that he could call her on the telephone. She wrote it down on paper for him and used hearts instead of zeros.

My father called my mother the very next night and the night after that and the night after that and the night after that and the night after that. They never got tired of talking to each other. After one year of talking to each other, my father took my mother on a lovely walk in the park one night. He stopped her where there was a beautiful view of a pond with moonlight shining down on it.

My father got down on one knee, pretending to tie his shoe, but my mother already knew what was coming, and her heart began to beat very fast.

My father looked up from his shoe into my mother's eyes and held up a ring. "Would you please marry me."

My mother said, "I would be very happy to," and they kissed each other. It was true love's kiss.

After that they got married, bought a house, and eventually had me.

According to my mother, I was the best part of it all.

\*\*\*

I like to think about that love story. It is a good one, probably the best one, actually. As for myself, I did not fall in love with Paul at first sight. I did not fall in love with Paul when I saw him comb his hair with his little black comb. I did not fall in love with Paul when he saved me from the snake with the poisonous-looking spots. I did not fall in love with Paul when he told the bullies at school to leave me alone.

Truthfully I have no idea when exactly I fell in love with Paul.

# Chapter 7

I always catch a cold in the summer. I don't know why, but it's true. Before Paula started sending letters to Paul, I did not know a single other person who caught colds in the summer. Everyone at school always caught their cold in the winter. In the winter, kids walked around coughing and sneezing and blowing their noses all day, and I bounced around as healthy as a bird. When summer came and all the children ran about playing, I felt miserable. Fortunately I was never sick for long. I could conquer a cold in two days.

Paula caught her cold at the same time as I caught mine, even though we were on separate ends of the country. I was at Paul's house with a runny nose and a horrible cough, and Paul was reading her letter. He said, "What do you know? Paula has a cold just like you, Maggie. Isn't that strange?"

I didn't feel too bad for Paula, to be honest. But I was interested that another person got sick in the summer like me.

Paula's cold and my cold were both caught just before the horrible announcement on the radio, but my cold was gone when I heard the announcement. I had already gotten better by then. I do not know how Paula felt when she heard the news. I would not be surprised if she felt better by then as well.

Here is the letter that Paula sent to Paul, where she told him about her cold:

*Dear Paul,*

 *I must be brief, because I do not feel well.*

 *I have caught a cold, even though it is summer. I always catch a cold in the summer it seems like. My nose feels like it has been stopped up, and I can only breathe if my mouth is open. My nose is doing that thing where, when I lie down to go to sleep, one side of my nose feels plugged, and if I roll over it switches to the other side of my nose. I think when I am a scientist, I will try to find a cure for the cold so no one will ever have to feel like this again. I think you will be a wonderful police scientist.*

 *I have asked my mother to go to the library to get the book you told me about. I am anxious to read it and, since I am sick, I will have nothing else to do. I am sure it will be good. It sounds wonderful.*

 *Let's be sure to do that when we become scientists.*

 *Love,*

 *Paula.*


Her letter was in response to the one Paul had written.

*Dear Paula,*

*I think I will become a scientist. You have convinced me. It sounds like a proper job for someone who wants to be smart like me.*

*My favorite book of all time is a book called* The Orphanage On Palmer Street, *by Reggie Zefu. I like the book so much that I love it, and I think you will too.*

*Do you know? Before, when people asked me what I wanted to do when I grew up, I always said I would like to be a police officer. The reason for this was that I wanted to protect good people. Being a cop takes a lot of bravery and a lot of guts and the badge is cool. I wonder if I could be both a police officer and a scientist? That would be the best thing. I would be called a "police scientist." I like the idea of that very much. I could protect people and do science at the same time. Do you think that is possible?*

*Snow is like ice, but it is better than ice because you can make snowmen and snowwomen out of it and you can build forts out of it and you can pick it up and eat it too. Snow tastes like a snow cone but without the syrup. It is very delicious and good for you.*

*When we are scientists we should try to find a way to make it snow everywhere, even in the desert, so that everyone can stand in it and see what fun it is.*

*That is all,*

*Love,*

*Paul.*

*Love, Paul?* was all I could think.

***

When the radio announced the horrible news, I was at Paul's house.

We had been listening to a show. It was a comedy show where two men argued with each other for half an hour about something or some other thing. Those two men had the funniest conversations. Everyone at school listened to them on the radio and would quote their favorite lines. The names of the men on the radio were Park and Maple. The show was called *The Park and Maple Half Hour*.

I thought the show was marvelous and that it should have been two hours long but Mother said that would be too long. "If it was two hours long," she said, "then there wouldn't be time to do anything else, and the entire night would be wasted."

I suppose she was right about that. Mother never did like Park and Maple. She didn't approve of arguing. She said it was unhealthy to listen to, and that is why I listened to the show at Paul's house. Mother knew I was listening to it at Paul's house. She didn't mind that. She just didn't want to hear it in her living room.

This night's show was exceptionally funny. Park was telling Maple, in his funny high-pitched voice, that he was tired of carrying groceries, so he wouldn't be going shopping anymore. Maple, the reasonable one with the low voice, told Park that there was simply no way that he could quit shopping. How would he get his food and necessities?

"It's easy," said Park. "I'll have you go shopping for me!"

"Me?" said Maple. "What makes you think I would do something like that?"

"What?" said Park. "It's only carrying groceries. What's so difficult about it, that you can't do it?"

"I could ask you the same thing," argued Maple. "No. It's out of the question. I won't carry your groceries for you. I have my dignity."

"Dignity?" cried Park. "You have dignity? Why, your socks don't even match!"

There was no way that we could know whether Maple's socks matched or not, but we all laughed at the idea of Maple sitting in front of a microphone with mismatched socks on.

"Now listen," Maple said, "there's no need to get personal about it. I just couldn't find a matching pair of socks this morning, that's all."

"Really I'm surprised at you, Maple," said Park. "And to think I was going to ask you to carry my groceries!"

"Oh," said Maple, "and who will you get to carry them, instead?"

"I'll ask the mailman."

"The mailman?"

"Yes," said Park, "the mailman. He stops at my house every day. He might as well bring me my groceries while he's at it."

What a funny idea, that a mailman would deliver groceries. How silly.

It was then that a strange voice, which was neither Park's nor Maple's, came on.

# Chapter 8

"We interrupt this program," said the strange new voice on the radio, "with really terrible news. We ask that all of the folks at home stay calm and not panic. We also ask that you do not rush to the hospital upon hearing the news, as it will do no good and only cause chaos.

"This is an official emergency broadcast.

"The virus known as the Durmon virus has, up to this point, been a perfectly harmless virus that has not bothered anyone, despite the fact that it infects us all. Unfortunately this afternoon an official report came in from a hospital in Trusband. The report detailed the sudden and unexpected death of a human being who had been in perfect health this very morning. After an examination done by doctors at the hospital, the cause of death was discovered to be the Durmon virus.

"Scientists were helicoptered to the hospital in Trusband to officially study the deceased, and to see what they could learn. They found that the virus had come out of its dormancy and begun to replicate itself, infecting and killing the cells that made up the heart of the deceased, causing sudden and instant death. The scientists then did an examination of a living resident at the hospital and found that the virus inside that resident was no longer dormant. It was actively killing the cells in the resident's heart. The resident claimed to feel no pain, save a slight discomfort in the chest.

"Within fifteen minutes that resident had perished, and so had one of the scientists.

"An official statement has been made by one of the scientists at the hospital, a woman named Dr. Henrietta Van Reeds. Dr. Van Reeds says that 'While the virus has, up to this point, been dormant, something seems to have stimulated it. The virus,' she says, 'is in the lytic phase now, and is attacking the hearts of all of the humans who are infected which, as we all know, is all of us. Some hearts are being attacked slower than others, and we are examining them to find out if there is any way to stop the virus.'

"Maggie Millburn, the scientist who famously discovered the virus over a decade ago, has vowed to come out of retirement to assist in finding a cure before the entire human race is wiped off the face of the earth.

"Godspeed, Mrs. Millburn. Godspeed.

"We now return to your regularly programed broadcast."

Park and Maple came back on, halfway through one of them asking the other if they had ever ridden a unicycle.

I looked at Paul, and Paul looked at me. Paul's mother stood up slowly and turned off the radio.

"Mom?" said Paul.

"I'm going to call your father," said Paul's mother. "Maggie, you ought to go home to your mother this instant."

I looked at Paul again.

"It really will be all right for us," he said. "Trust me."

I trusted Paul completely, so I knew that I could go home and everything would be all right. I ran out of Paul's house to my bike and pedaled it as fast as my legs would go.

As I pedaled my bike home, I started to cry. This was one of the last times I ever cried. It wasn't the very last time I cried, but it was one of the last times.

I was crying because I was scared. I thought about the virus inside me, killing the cells in my heart. I put one hand on my chest and felt my heart beat. It was beating very fast, partly because I was riding so fast, and partly because I was so frightened.

*How could my heart be infected by a virus? Am I going to die?* was all I could think.

I was so afraid that I would die before I saw my mother again. I was scared that my heart would break as I rode home, and that I would fall over and blink a few times and then never blink again.

"Help," is what I whispered as I rode home, "help."

The people in the houses I passed by were all rushing about as well, many of them were running out to the street, getting in their cars, and driving away. I didn't know where they were going that night, but I learned later that they had all been going to the hospital. Apparently that night hundreds of people went to the hospital near my house and many of them died trying to get through the doors. Some died because of the Durmon virus, and others were just trampled by all the frightened people.

When I got to my house, I was drenched in sweat. It really was so hot, even though the sun was down. I could barely breathe and my heart was racing. I kept my hand on my heart as I ran inside and found my mother. She was sitting on the couch with her notebook out. She was trying to write a poem. When she heard me come in, she said, "Can you think of any word that rhymes with 'leaves'?"

"Mother," I said to her, but I was sobbing.

She instantly put down her notebook and came to me.

"What is it, sweetie," she said to me very gently, wrapping her arms around me even though I was hot.

"Mother," I said again, gasping for air, "help."

My mother ran into the kitchen and got two glasses of water. She gave one of them to me and the other she poured over my head, spilling water all over the carpet. The water was cold and it cooled me off a lot. I took a drink of the water in the cup I held, and then I took a deep breath so that I wouldn't sob so much, and I told her the awful news.

"The Durmon virus," I said. "The man on the radio said that it's killing people by killing all the cells in their heart."

Mother turned on the radio and tuned it to a news station. She heard the news for herself. Even more people had died since the emergency broadcast I had heard at Paul's house, including Park and Maple. Apparently just after Paul's mother turned off the radio, Park fell back in his chair, dead, and Maple screamed, only to fall over dead himself moments later. The news reporter told us that Park and Maple's dead bodies were found leaning on each other in their chairs. He said that Maple had apparently reached for Park's head when Park had died, and that one of Maple's hands was resting around Park's shoulder.

Mother did a thing as she heard this where she put one hand over her mouth. She looked very shocked and worried when she did that.

"Mother," I said, "am I going to die?"

That was a selfish thing to ask. I don't think I should have asked that. I wish I hadn't.

\*\*\*

The next day my mother would not let me leave the house. I was not happy about this because I wanted to see Paul, but I agreed to it. Mother believed that at any moment, one of us would die. Seeing her so worried made me feel very worried myself. I think she wanted me to stay home because she wanted to be there if I died, so that I wouldn't be alone when it happened. When I thought about mother dying in front of me, however, I was very scared. I did not want that to happen. I did not want to see her die. That is one of the reasons I wanted to leave the house. The other reason was that I did not know whether Paul was alive or dead, and that made me very worried. I wanted to check on him.

Mother sat in front of the radio all day listening to updates that came every half-hour, but they were not really updates since nothing new was happening. The updates only told that more people were dying, and that they were dying all over the world.

***

After lunch I had had enough of the doom and gloom, and so I went up to my room. I looked out my window, but I could not see Paul's house from there. I imagined Paul sitting in the attic, looking out the little round window at the street below. I imagined him combing his hair with his little black comb. His small face fit the window perfectly.

Then I imagined something terrible: Paul falling over and dying alone in his attic. I was so worried for Paul that I decided to pray. Mother had been telling me to pray all morning, and I still hadn't done it yet.

I don't really like to pray because sometimes I think, *What if God isn't listening to me?* If he isn't listening, then I'm just kneeling and talking to nobody in particular, and that makes me feel silly. I hope God listens. I really hope He listens.

I knelt beside my bed, which had blue covers, and I said a prayer.

"Dear God," I said, "please protect Paul, and do not let the virus kill him. Protect Mother too. And protect me. It doesn't make sense if I die. If I die, I won't get to stay with Paul and Mother. That's why You've got to protect all three of us. That way we can stay together. I don't want any of us to get separated.

"I'm sorry I'm not always very good, by the way. Please help me to listen to what Mother says. I do try to be good. Why can't I just be good? Why do I not listen to mother? Did You make me this way? Why would You do something like that? Do You know?

"Anyway please help me to be brave like Paul. I'm sure if Paul is still alive, that he is being very brave right now. He is probably telling his mother not to worry.

"Anyways, amen."

When I was finished praying, I did feel a little bit better.

I looked in my room for something to distract myself with. Whenever I wasn't distracted by something, I started to feel my chest, and when I started doing that, I always thought I could feel the virus killing me. I had felt that way all night and all morning.

I looked at my dolls, which were all sitting in a row in their dresses. Their eyes were creepy. When I went to sleep at night, I always put them in my closet, so they wouldn't stare at me.

I looked at my bookshelf, but I had read all of the books on there, and I hate to reread things because I already know how they end. It's no fun to read something when you know how it ends. That's what I think.

If only someone wrote a book that had a different ending every time you read it. Wouldn't that be something? If you didn't like how it ended the first time, you could simply read it again, and it would be all new. That would be a good book. And if you liked the characters, you could keep reading it and seeing them do different things until you found the perfect ending.

Well, I decided there in my room that I ought to write a book with an ending that changed every time.

I got a pencil and a piece of lined paper out of my desk and sat down and began to write.

This is what I wrote: This book is a book that ends differently every time, so that you can read it again and again. It is a story about an explorer who discovers buried treasures all over the world. The explorer's name is Zola Taylor, like the singer. I am calling her this because I wish my name was Zola Taylor.

Zola Taylor looks a lot like I do, except she is grown-up and very beautiful.

This is a story about a time when Zola explored an island in the ocean.

Zola went to an island in the ocean because she heard there was treasure there. When she got to the island, it was very hot. Zola got right to digging in the sand because she knew that treasure is always buried in the sand.

As she dug she realized that the island was actually a volcano, and it was about to explode. Zola ran to her boat and started to sail away, but it was too late. The volcano erupted.

Hot lava fell out of the sky all around Zola. She sped her boat away as fast as she could, but one of the pieces of the lava hit the boat and it sank.

Zola went underwater and opened her eyes. She realized, then and there, that she could breathe underwater.

Zola looked around and saw beautiful fish. Some fish were sparkly and green, some fish were flat and blue, some fish were fat and round with spikes on their heads, some fish had swords for noses, some fish had large black eyes, some fish had large tails that swished, and some fish swam right up to Zola and kissed her arms and face to welcome her to the ocean.

*It is very nice down here,* thought Zola, *and it is very quiet too. And nobody ever dies of a virus underneath the water. Here in the ocean, everything is fine.*

Zola swam and swam and made friends with many fish.

Finally she was bored of just swimming, and so she decided to do some exploring under the water. When she swam down to the bottom of the ocean, she found a lot of shipwrecks. In the ships there were chests full of gold and diamonds. Zola showed the jewels to the fish and explained to them how valuable the diamonds and gold were.

The fish did not really understand Zola, but they nodded and listened to her.

Zola liked to talk underwater because bubbles came out of her mouth as she talked. The bubbles tickled Zola's nose, and so she started to laugh, which made more and more bubbles come out, until she was rolling around in the water just laughing. She was very happy.

When Zola had explored long enough, she found what she was looking for. She found an underwater volcano on the bottom of the ocean. As she swam closer, the water got very hot, but Zola's skin could withstand it. She got right up close to the volcano and looked inside.

Inside the volcano there was lava that came right up and touched the water without cooling off. It was that hot. There were special fish inside the volcano that Zola had never seen before. These fish could withstand the heat just the way Zola could. They had the same kind of thick skin.

These fish were interesting, indeed. They were red fish with very long narrow bodies, which they wiggled back and forth to move. The fish all swam with their mouths opened, and so it looked to Zola as if they were panting.

There were also large crabs in the volcano that were almost as big as Zola herself.

Zola was amazed by what she had found.

\*\*\*

I stopped writing because no matter how hard I tried, I couldn't think of a way to make it end differently every time.

# Chapter 9

I went down to dinner that night and told my mother that I wanted to go to the library.

"Why do you want to do that?" Mother asked. "I thought you hated the library."

"Because I want to get a book," I said.

It was true. I did want to get a book. I wanted to get *The Orphanage on Palmer Street*. It was the book Paul had said was his favorite in his letter to Paula. I wanted to read it to find out why Paul liked it so much. I thought that if I could find out why he liked it, I could add what he liked to my book about Zola, so that he would like my book too.

Mother didn't want to take me to the library at all.

"Please Mother, please," I said. "If we go, I promise I'll be very obedient for the rest of my life. I swear."

"No," said Mother. "It's dangerous. I want to stay in the house. I don't want to go out, and I don't want you to go out either."

"But Mother," I said, "if we don't go out soon, we'll die in here."

After I said that, I felt bad that I had said it. Mother put her hand over her mouth when she heard me. She gasped too. She looked at me, and her eyes sort of got tears in them.

"I'm sorry," I said, looking down at my plate.

"No," said Mother, and she stood up and walked around the table to where I was sitting. She wrapped her arms around me, "It's OK," she said.

I was embarrassed because I knew my mother was crying, and I didn't know what to do. I held onto her hand and started to cry myself, just because I was embarrassed.

Mother stayed with me like that for a long time, not saying anything, but shaking a little because she was crying.

I think Mother was sad because I said that we would die. Maybe she was sad because she hadn't wanted me to know so much about death yet.

That's something that Paul told me. He said his parents never listened to the radio when he was around, because they didn't want him to know what was going on. He said he overheard them talking one night after he was supposed to be in bed but had snuck out to get a drink of water. They were in the kitchen whispering, and Paul just sat there and listened to them from around the corner.

Paul's mother said to Paul's father, "He's too young to be hearing about the virus, it will upset him. We mustn't let him hear a word of it. He is only a child. He will not understand. Children aren't supposed to know about death and dying and things like that. It is unhealthy for them to think about it."

"We'll have to keep the radio off when he's around," said Paul's father. "You'll have to watch him closely to make sure he doesn't sneak around trying to find out things behind our back. I don't trust him. He's too inquisitive for his own good."

"I will watch him," is what Paul's mother said.

At that point Paul got too frightened that they would find him listening, and so he snuck back upstairs to his bedroom.

Both Paul and I had known about death for a long time before the announcement. We learned about it by ourselves when we were at the park one time.

*** 

The park in our neighborhood had a trail next to it, which went into the woods in a big circle and then came back to the park. Paul and I walked on this trail. There was a tree that we knew of that we liked to climb because it was very big, and there was a spot for Paul, and a spot for me on it.

We walked on that trail one day because we were going to visit our tree, but before we got to there, we found a squirrel lying on the ground. It wasn't moving.

"Is it sleeping?" I asked Paul.

"I'll wake it up," said Paul. "It is dangerous for it to sleep here, where any dog could pick it up and bite it."

Paul poked the squirrel in the shoulder with a long stick, but the squirrel did not budge. He poked it again and still it did not budge. Finally Paul turned the squirrel over with the stick, and we saw that its eyes were wide-open.

"Is it sick?" I asked.

"No," said Paul. "I think it might be dead."

Paul had read books like *Robin Hood* and *The Count of Monte Cristo*, so he knew a bit more about death than I did.

"How did it die?" I asked.

"It was probably shot with an arrow," said Paul, "or it got stabbed in the stomach during a sword fight."

"Wow," I said. Before then we had both heard people talk about death in conversations. I had heard my mother talk to her friend about her grandfather who "passed away," and Paul had read his books, but neither of us had ever seen it up close before.

It was frightening to see a dead animal. The squirrel's eyes were wide-open, but it wasn't looking at anything. No matter how hard we poked it, it wouldn't move.

"What should we do with it?" I asked Paul. "It wouldn't be right to leave the poor dear here."

"We should have a funeral," said Paul. "That is what they do with people who die."

"How do we do that?" I asked.

"We dig a hole," said Paul, "and we put the squirrel in it, and then we fill the hole up, and then we put a rock on top of the place where we buried it. That way, we always remember where it is."

The rest of the day at the park was spent beside the

nature trail, digging. We didn't have a shovel, so we used sticks. It was not too hard to dig because the dirt was muddy from a rainstorm that happened two days earlier.

When the hole was big enough, Paul put the squirrel inside it. He didn't pick it up with his hands but carried it with two sticks. We had both been told by our mothers that we should never touch a wild animal, because they might have diseases.

After we buried the squirrel, we put a rock on the spot and promised to come visit it next week.

When we came back the next week, the rock had been moved and the hole had been dug up. The squirrel was gone.

When I got home, I asked my mother what she thought might have happened. She said that a dog had probably smelled the dead squirrel and dug it up then taken it away so that it could roll on it.

"Why would a dog roll on a dead squirrel?" I asked.

"Because dogs don't have any sense," said my mother.

That made me laugh. When I was done laughing my mother said to me, "If you find any more dead animals in the woods, just leave them be."

# Chapter 10

After three days of being stuck in the house with nobody but Mother, there was a speech on the radio. The speech was given by a woman with a very soothing voice.

"Listen," she said, "three days ago a tragedy occurred: The Durmon virus began to kill people. Due to the nature of the virus's attack, people have called it, 'The Heartbreak Virus.' What it does is it breaks down the cells in the heart of its host, until the heart stops beating and the host dies. Currently there is no cure, and currently everyone is infected.

"It has been brought to our attention that because of this outbreak, people have looted, rioted, quit their jobs, and done other rash things.

"I am here to encourage you all to stay calm, and to return to living your lives as normally as you did before the outbreak. This is all that we can do now, and it is better than doing nothing. Maggie Millburn, and a team of gifted scientists are at work, right now, trying to find a cure. The second one is found, it will be released to the world for a reasonable price, so that everyone will have access to it.

"Please listen, hiding in your house or running about looting is doing no good. You have all got to return to your jobs. Production must continue so that when the cure is found, we have the means to send it out to everyone. Don't you see? It is for your own good.

"Next week there will be a special interview with Maggie Millburn, where she will discuss the progress of finding a cure and also tell us a bit more about the technicalities of the virus. For now, please, calm down and do your part. The human race is at stake."

I liked the woman's voice. She sounded very sweet.

Mother had listened to the announcement with a very serious expression on her face. I could tell she was thinking about it. I watched her sit there and when I got tired of the quiet, I finally said, "Mother, may I go ride my bike to Paul's house?"

Mother looked at me as if I had woken her from a heavy sleep. "I don't like this," she said, but it seemed as if she was talking to herself and not to me. "I don't like this one bit."

Mother stood up and walked into the kitchen. She opened up the cupboards and removed a half-eaten loaf of bread.

"Please, Mother," I said, standing in the doorway between the living room and the kitchen, "I'll go very quickly on my pink bike, and I'll come right back. I want to see Paul."

Mother sighed, which was a good sign. She always sighed if she was about to give in. "If you come right back," she said.

I practically screamed I was so excited.

"And you've got to be quick." She added, "If you start to feel pain in your chest, you must come right back home, even if you haven't made it to Paul's house yet."

"I will, I will, I will," I said, as I put my sandals on.

*** 

To finally see Paul put me in a good mood. I ran out to the garage and hopped on my bike faster than a racehorse. Then I stopped, ran back inside, and grabbed what I had written about Zola, and ran back out to the garage.

I rode to Paul's house at top speed, even though it felt as if it was hotter today than ever before. It felt as if it was a million degrees outside. I could feel heat coming off the pavement. I could feel sweat on my back.

At Paul's house I knocked quietly on the door. I was suddenly afraid that there wouldn't be any answer because they had all died or something. I held my breath and shuddered, and then suddenly Paul's mother was in the doorway ushering me inside.

"Well, look who is here," she said. "Paul will be so pleased. I'll call him down for you."

I was so happy to hear that Paul hadn't bit the dust that I said, "I'll just go up and surprise him if you don't mind, ma'am."

Paul's mother didn't mind and even if she did, she didn't say so. I ran up the stairs clomping my feet because I was in such a hurry.

When I got to his room, I opened the door, but he wasn't there, so I knew he was in the attic, which was just where I envisioned him being. I pulled down the trap door and climbed the ladder. When my head poked above the floor of the attic, I saw him by the window. He was combing his hair with his little black comb and thinking.

"Hi-o, Paul," I said cheerfully because I was so happy to see him.

Paul turned around with a start; I think because he recognized my voice.

"Maggie!" he said with a smile, and then he turned very serious. "You'd better not have come without your mother's permission. Even if you did, it's still nice to see you again. Hasn't it been dull these past few days?"

"I've been having a perfectly dreadful time," I told Paul.

"Have you been listening to the radio?"

"Yes, I have," I said, walking across the attic and sitting down next to him. "It's so boring. There's never anything fun like Park and Maple on anymore. It's all about the Durmon virus, now. I didn't know that anybody could talk for so long about just one thing, and it isn't even a thing that anybody likes! I think the radio should talk about things people like, to cheer us up. That's what I think."

"They can't do that," said Paul. "They have to tell us what's happening, so that we aren't confused. They are providing the news. They do it because people want to know what's going on."

"I don't know," I said. "I mean, I know what's going on, and I'd really rather not. It's just awful, Paul, hundreds of thousands of people are dying every day, and you never know who could be next."

"That's terrible," said Paul. "I didn't know."

"Yes, well it's all over the radio," I said. I was proud of myself for knowing something that Paul didn't know, because usually he was telling me something that I didn't know. Paul did that a lot. He liked to explain things.

One time when we were in his backyard, I found a little thing that looked an awful lot like a mushroom. I told Paul I was going to eat it, but he told me not to. He told me it was poisonous. Paul was always ruining the fun like that. It made me feel so stupid, standing there holding a poisonous mushroom about to eat it. I blushed and felt very hot and threw the mushroom on the ground. I was so embarrassed.

# Chapter 11

I showed Paul my book about Zola, and he was impressed. He told me that he liked it because Zola could breathe underwater, and that was something he wished he could do. He said that was a fine kind of book. He said that most books were just stories about people who did things that the readers wished they could do.

When he told me that, I thought maybe I should make Zola fly too, because I always wanted to fly.

Wouldn't flying be so much fun? If I could fly, I would go up as high as I could go, all the way to the top of the sky, and then I would dive down and make the biggest splash that anyone had ever seen at the community pool. If only there were still people around to go to the community pool to see my splash.

After Paul read my book a few times and made a few corrections for me, he tried to help me think of a way to make it end differently every time.

"Do you think it's impossible?" I asked.

"No," said Paul. "I don't think it's impossible. I think we just haven't thought of it yet."

Suddenly Paul's mother's head appeared in the entrance to the attic. "Hello," said Paul's mother's head.

"Hello," said Paul.

"Hello," I said.

"The mail just arrived, and there's a letter for you, Paul," said Paul's mother's head.

Paul's mother lifted an arm through the trap door and placed a letter on the floor, then she vanished from sight.

"Is it from Paula?" I asked, trying to hide my annoyance.

"Probably," said Paul, running to the little envelope and scooping it up.

He tore open the envelope and began to read eagerly.

*Dear Paul,*

*I am so worried, Paul. I am really frightened. People are dying like crazy. A lot of my family has died. My aunt and my uncle died, and my cousins did too. I'm very scared. We couldn't even go to the funeral. I wanted to go because I've never been to a funeral before, but mother said I could not go.*

*Mother walks around wearing a stethoscope now. She is always listening to her own heartbeat. She claims she can hear the virus inside her heart, eating away at her cells. She says it sounds like termites. She says it sounds like the virus has a little pick and hammer, and that it is just picking away.*

*I was too afraid to ask her to listen to my heart. I was worried she would hear them in me too. Oh Paul, I hope you're alive. If you've died, I think I'll cry for the rest of my life. Please write to me as soon as you get this letter, so that I know you're safe.*

*We have to write to each other because we are all that we've got now, OK, Paul? Promise me that you will write to me. Really promise.*

*Enclosed with this letter is a picture of me. I didn't have a picture of just me so I cut it out of a family photo in our photo album. It is a recent picture, but I did get a nasty scratch on my elbow after it was taken, so I don't look exactly the same now. Please send me a picture of yourself, that way we both know what the other one looks like, and we can find one another no matter where we end up.*

*Oh I do hope you are still alive. I really do.*

*I haven't had time to think since all this started.*

*Love,*

*Paula.*


The picture of Paula that had been cut out of her family photo was about the size of the palm of my hand. Paula was sitting down, and you could really only see the top half of her. She had red hair and blue eyes, and her teeth were impossibly straight. Her smile made her look very happy, which is how it should look, you know? She was wearing a purple sweater in the photo that was baggy, but she still looked awfully happy, nonetheless.

Paul was very happy with the picture.

"This is exactly how I thought she'd look," he said. "I should write her a letter immediately, so she doesn't worry too much."

I was mad at Paula because she had told Paul all of the things that I had wanted to tell him the whole time that I was stuck at home. I had been just as worried as Paula was about Paul, and whether he was alive or not. Yet for some reason, all that Paul cared about was Paula and her letters. He had completely forgotten about Zola and my book, which ends differently every time.

"Paul," I said, "don't you think you should help me think of a way to make the book end differently every time, before you write Paula back? After all, I was here first."

Paul already had a pen and a piece of paper and was writing away.

"Do you know what?" said Paul. "We ought to ask Paula if she can think of a way to make a book end differently every time you read it. Paula is very smart. She's bound to know of a way. I'll mention it to her." And then Paul said to me, "Maggie, if you don't mind, could you go down and ask my mother if she has any recent photographs of me that I could send to Paula? It would save me the trouble."

"No," I said. "I don't want to do that."

I sat with my arms folded and watched him write, determined to never do anything he asked me to ever again, but then I got bored, so I went downstairs and asked his mother if she had any photos of Paul.

"What does he want the photo for?" she asked.

"Oh," I said casually, "it's just silly, ma'am. It's the silliest thing. Paula sent him a photo of herself in this letter he just got, and she asked him to send one of himself so that she can know what he looks like. Isn't that just silly?"

"Oh," said Paul's mother, "that's very sweet. It's like they're a tiny little couple."

"Don't say that!" I screamed at her. "Don't you ever say that!"

Paul's mother looked startled. She had never seen me raise my voice before. I have a very loud voice. My mother always said I did. "No, I don't!" is what I would shout at her when she said this. She would always act as if she was deaf after I did that. She would put her little finger in her ear and wiggle it around and then go, "Eh? Eh? Eh?" until I was laughing so hard I fell over. The only way to make her stop going, "Eh? Eh? Eh?" was to get really close to her ear and scream, "Mother, can you hear me now?" Then she would put her hands over her ears and go, "Ow."

Paul's mother took out her family photo album and flipped through the pictures. She was quiet, and I was quiet, and we both felt awkward about how I had screamed at her.

I'm sure she was upset. After all, children are not supposed to scream at adults. I know that much.

Finally she said to me, "Maggie, which picture should we use?"

She showed me a few options. There was one picture of Paul which was him standing on the porch in his blue shorts, sandals, and a striped T-shirt. He looked like a little sailor with his hair all combed. The picture made my stomach feel warm and cozy. I definitely didn't want Paula to get that picture. Next she showed me a picture of Paul from Christmas. He was in a new pair of red pajamas, and he was opening a present, which was a book about bugs. The last picture she showed me was a picture of him dressed in a little suit. It was taken right before they left for Sunday School. In this picture, Paul looked uncomfortable because his collar was too tight. He was not smiling but instead just staring at the camera. He looked as if he was saying, "I don't want to go. I feel like an idiot."

When I saw that picture, I started to giggle.

It was not a very good picture, I promise, and so of course it was the one I told Paul's mother to use.

"Are you sure?" she asked, as she flipped back to the one where he looked like a sailor. "I really like this one. Don't you think Paula will like it?"

In my head I was thinking this the whole time, *I don't want Paula to like it. I want her to hate Paul so much that she never writes him a letter again. I want her to die. I want her to die. Why won't the Durmon virus just kill her?*

After I thought this, I felt very bad. I know it was only a thought, but I should not have thought it. I should have stopped my brain from thinking it. It was an awful thing to think.

"Yes," Paul's mother was saying, "yes, let's use this one."

She gave me the picture of Paul in his shorts where he looked like a sailor, and I slowly took it up the stairs to him.

# Chapter 12

The letter that Paul wrote to Paula really rubbed me the wrong way. I did not like it at all. It annoyed me very much. And when I showed the picture of Paul that his mother had selected, he was so pleased with it.

"This is a very good picture of me," he said so matter-of-factly. I hate that. I can't stand somebody who likes the way they look in pictures.

There were very popular girls at our school who all had blond hair and cherry-flavored lip gloss that they could put on whenever they felt like, and they were always so proud of their own pictures. They would bring pictures of themselves to show off to everyone else. And the pictures were pretty good too. The girls' eyes sparkled in the pictures. They always sparkled. Those nasty girls had the most stunning blue eyes. They were so stunning I wanted to puke.

I hate to see a picture of myself. I think to myself, *Wow Maggie, your eyes are too big and they don't sparkle at all. Your ears are too big too, and your teeth aren't straight at all. It's really pathetic.* That is how everyone should see their own pictures.

***

Those blond girls with their cherry-flavored lip gloss are all gone now. Every last one of them.

***

The fact is, it was a very good photo of Paul, and he knew it. He was happy to send it to Paula. He really wanted to make a good impression. I didn't like that one bit.

"Dearest Paula," is how Paul's letter to her started. He had written "dearest" and then crossed out the "est" part and then written it back in. He was sure thorough.

*Dearest Paula,*

*Do not worry, Paula. I am OK. I am happy to hear from you. I was worried about you. This letter shall be sent out as soon as it is possible to do so. I want you to know that I am fine, and my heart has not broken yet.*

*I think the world is a really scary place. I'm scared to just be alive these days because I could die at any moment. It is so frightening to realize that you could die at any moment all because of a little virus.*

*I hope your mother is all right. She does not sound sane, does she? No, she sounds like she has completely lost her mind. How could a virus make a noise anyway? Anyway, you should keep me updated so that I can be of service if I need to.*

*Here's something to take your mind off your troubles. I have a friend named Maggie, who is writing a book about an explorer named Zola. She wants the ending of the book to be different every time you read it, so that people will read it over and over again. Do you know how to make an ending for a book that is different every time you read it? If you can think of something please let Maggie and I know. Thank you.*

*I'm sending a picture of myself with the letter, so that you can see what I look like. I hope you like it. It isn't a very good picture.*

"Liar," I said when I read this part. "You said you thought it was a very good picture just a moment ago."

"Yes," agreed Paul. "But if I tell her that it is not a very good picture, then she will think I am even more handsome."

"Why do you care if she thinks you're more handsome, or not?" I asked, getting very angry.

This stumped Paul, and I'm glad it did. It served him right. He looked at the picture and the letter, and finally said, "I don't want to seem like I am bragging, and so I am saying it isn't very good out of humility."

It was not an excuse I could argue with because Paul was very humble for most of the time. Paul didn't go on and on about how great he was. Sometimes Paul's father would brag about himself, but never Paul.

One time I stayed at Paul's house for dinner, and Paul's father talked on and on about how well the business was doing, and it was all thanks to him.

"I really don't know what they'd do without me," he said to Paul's mother in between big bites of meatloaf. "You know I saved them ten hours of labor today by employing a new system for doing the paperwork. It gets the work done twice as fast. The boys in sales were so impressed they bought me lunch! A big, fat, juicy stinking burger. It was so good because I really deserved it, you know? Business is all about savoring the things that you earn because you deserve them. I feel very pampered today, dear. It was such a relief to not have to eat the same ham on wheat bread atrocity you send with me every day. Boy, I really am something, you know that? I really am something."

I don't like meatloaf, but I don't like Paul's father even more.

***

The letter to Paula went on:

*It isn't a very good picture.*
*Have you had a chance to read* The Orphanage on Palmer Street, *yet? I am curious to know your thoughts.*

*With love,*
*Paul.*

After Paul mailed his letter to Paula, he and I played pirates in the attic. We got into a really intense cannon fight in this play. It was a battle on the open sea in the middle of a ferocious storm, but it was really all just pretend.

Both Paul and I were running up and down the sides of our ships, firing cannon balls at each other while waves splashed over the side and threatened to sweep us off our feet. It was good fun.

When I suddenly remembered that I had promised Mother I would be home soon, I told Paul I had to go and rode back home as fast as I could.

I found mother on the couch asleep. The radio was on and, for once, it wasn't talking about the virus. It was playing some pretty piano music.

I used to take piano lessons. If I see a piano, I can play a few songs but I'm not very good. I just need a little practice is all. Whoever was playing the piano on the radio was very good. I closed my eyes and listened to it. The music made me spin around the living room with my arms stretched out. It was that kind of piano music. When the song ended I stopped spinning and opened my eyes.

Mother was watching me. I felt embarrassed, but she just smiled.

"You are a little ballerina girl," she told me.

# Chapter 13

Riding in the car is nice because if it is hot out, you can roll down the windows and the air blowing in feels cool. If it is snowing, you can turn on the heat and feel cozy and warm in your own seat. On the day that Mother took me to the library it was very hot, and so we rolled down all the windows.

Mother was a very good driver. She told me that the trick to being a good driver was that you had to always be careful, and to go slower rather than faster. She would then say that that was true about every aspect of life. No matter what you were doing, it was best to be careful, and to go slower rather than faster.

The library was a large red brick building in the middle of town. It had big windows in it that went all the way to the ceiling and all the way to the floor. These windows were fun to look out, because you felt as if you were on a spaceship looking at outer space. Or you could feel like an animal at the zoo if you wanted to.

When Mother and I went into the library, it was our first time to be out in public since the outbreak. We both felt awkward, as if we were being stared at by everyone. "Stay calm," my mother told me, and she took my hand.

We walked through the library to where there was a desk with an old woman sitting behind it. The old woman was in a blue sweater and navy blue pants. Her hair was so white. It was the whitest hair I had ever seen, and it was all fluffy too. Her hair was like a cotton ball. She had lots of wrinkles on her face, and her neck hung down and wobbled. She was wearing a pair of glasses with square lenses, and there was a thin gold chain attached to the glasses that went behind her neck so that she could wear her glasses as a necklace if she wanted to.

This old woman was the person who helped you find the books you were looking for. She had worked at the library for so long that she could tell where a book was if you just asked her.

"Excuse me," I said shyly, "do you know where *The Orphanage on Palmer Street* is located?"

The old woman sat there and shivered for a moment. Then she stood up and said, "Come with me, darling."

I followed her and Mother followed me, and together we all ended up where the book was. The copy of the book the library had was old, and a bit chewed in one corner, but it would do the trick.

"Yes, please," I said. "I will take it."

The book had a lovely cover. It was a drawn picture of a stony street with buildings in the background. The buildings were made of stone too, and there were yellow lights glowing out of the windows. Coming out of the sidewalk, there was a sign which said, "Palmer St." on it.

"So this is Palmer Street," I thought as I looked at the picture on the cover. Above that sign were words printed in yellow that said, *The Orphanage on*, so you had to finish the title by looking at the street sign below. It was very creative. At the bottom of the book in smaller yellow writing it said, "Written by Reggie Zefu."

And if you looked very closely at one of the buildings at the back of the drawing, you could see a little boy with brown hair, peeking his eyes over the fence.

*That boy must be in the story,* I thought. And though I could only see his eyes, sort of, he seemed very nice, and he seemed as if he really wanted me to read about him.

The old woman led us back to the table so that she could stamp the book for us. She was the kind of old lady who walked with a waddle. She swayed from side to side with each step. Her head leaned one way and then the other. It reminded me of a swing set.

As she led us along, I heard her moan softly. It was such a soft moan, I wasn't sure if I had heard it at all.

When the old woman put her hand over her heart and fell over my mother moved very quickly. The first thing my mother did when the old woman fell down was to cover my eyes with her hands. She screamed for help next, and I could hear footsteps and voices shouting. I could not see anything because of Mother's hands.

Mother dragged me out of the library as fast as she could, and she kept her hands over my eyes the whole time. I couldn't see a thing. I didn't know where I was, or where I was going. I just followed where Mother guided me. I was scared, because Mother didn't usually behave like this. I felt weird and embarrassed and really frightened.

When we got to the car, Mother turned it on and left the parking lot as quickly as she could. Down the road a few blocks, an ambulance passed us going in the opposite direction, going toward the library.

"Is everything all right?" I asked Mother.

"Everything is fine, darling," said Mother. Her hair was messed up on the side. It was sticking up. She looked a little crazy like that. She looked as if she had fallen asleep on the couch in the middle of the day.

When I looked down, I realized that I had taken the book without getting it stamped. I had stolen it. It wasn't really my fault, of course. I had a pair of hands over my eyes. How could I see anything?

"Mother, we didn't check this out," I said, holding up the book. "Should we go back?"

"No," she told me. "We are never going back to that library again."

When I got home, I went to my room. I took the book with me. I still have that book to this day. I have never taken it back. There is no one at the library to take it back to anymore, so I don't think I need to do that.

As for the old woman, I think that what happened in the library that day was that that old woman died of the Durmon virus. Yes, I am fairly confident that that is what happened. She grabbed her chest right where her heart would be, and then she fell down. I didn't see anymore after that, but I don't think it could be anything else.

I don't know why people called it "dying of heartbreak." That seems like such a cruel joke. There is nobody to call it "dying of heartbreak" now. Nobody but me.

# Chapter 14

On the day of the interview with Maggie Millburn, everybody turned on their radios. Paul's parents even let Paul listen to this. They had realized that Paul would need to know what was happening in case both of them died and Paul didn't. I thought that was a smart thing to do for Paul, and it must have been his mother who suggested it. I cannot imagine that Paul's father suggested anything that reasonable. Paul's father was beginning to show signs of insanity at that point.

Mother and I sat close to the radio and waited for six o'clock to arrive. I was excited to hear Maggie Millburn because I was named after her. It would be like listening to a past version of myself.

At six o'clock on the dot, the interview began. The person interviewing Maggie Millburn was the same woman with the soothing voice who had told everyone to stop panicking the week before. Her name was Susan Cathalon. She was becoming very popular on the radio because of her soothing voice.

She began the interview by introducing Maggie Millburn and explaining some of the history of how Maggie discovered the disease.

The first question Susan asked Maggie was, "Have you found a cure?"

"No," said Maggie sadly, and her voice frightened me. Maggie Millburn had one of those old crinkly voices that sounds scratchy, like sandpaper. "No," said Maggie, "we still have not found anything that kills the virus. Everything we have tried has failed. We have begun to search for people who are immune to the virus. Some of the scientists think that, given the amount of people there are, surely there is someone out there who cannot be harmed by it. If we can find this human before they are the last one left, we may be able to find out what makes them immune and use that to create the cure."

"Fascinating," said Susan in such a way that I could envision her nodding her head. I could see her earrings swinging back and forth as she nodded. Her voice was descriptive like that. When she spoke, you could see her even if you couldn't really. You could see her in your mind.

"Do you think, Mrs. Millburn, that you will be able to find someone who is immune in time to save the human race?"

"No," said Maggie. She almost seemed to be shouting her answers so that she could be understood above the horrid crackling in her voice. "No, I don't think we can find someone in time. I think there are too many people in the world and not enough hospitals and centers who can do the necessary testing to find such an individual. Especially when the amount of people in the world grows shorter every day, that means fewer people who are trained in the medical field. Our chances of survival continue to go down with the total number of people alive on the planet."

"We must not give up hope," said Susan before asking the next question. "Mrs. Millburn, when you discovered the virus all those years ago, why did you name it Durmon?"

Maggie Millburn was quiet long enough that I thought the radio had turned off. When she did speak, she spoke softly.

"Well," she said, "I had always wanted a child, a little boy that I could name Durmon. Unfortunately I never married and so I named that virus the Durmon virus, because it was my baby. I found it and I took care of it. I loved it as if it were my own child. I spent my life studying it and trying to figure out why it was there, inside everyone like that."

"What do you think about the virus now? Now that it is no longer dormant but is killing so many people?"

"I think," said Maggie, "that the virus is being a very bad boy. And I wish I could stop it before it hurts anyone else."

"Now there are some," said Susan, "who believe that this virus is planet earth's way of removing humans from existence because we cause so much damage, what with wars and bombs and plastic. What do you make of this idea?"

"What idea?"

"The idea that this virus is planet earth's way of eradicating all of humanity to save nature."

"Oh," said Maggie, "well, I suppose it is possible. And if it is the planet's way of killing us all, it's doing a very good job at it."

***

Personally I do not think that the virus was made by planet earth to kill all of humanity. If that were the case, I would not still be here. I would be dead just like everybody else.

***

But I am still here.

***

After that, Maggie explained what we were all supposed to do in order to get tested. If one of us was found to be immune to the virus, we would be flown out to the lab where Maggie and the other scientists worked, and we would be used to make a cure.

When people heard that there was a chance that they might be immune, they all came running. Everybody figured that, since they had lasted this long, surely they were the special one.

At our local hospital, it was so crowded that you couldn't get within two miles of the place. Cars filled up the road and blocked all the traffic. People were hitchhiking there to get tested.

Mother did not want to take me, but it was required. Every citizen of the world was to be tested. That was the only way that someone with an immunity could be found.

My mother and I drove toward the hospital, but we had to get out and walk the last two miles. I did not know just how long two miles was to walk until I had to walk it with Mother in that awful, awful heat.

Do you know? The heat was so hot that it felt as if I was in hell? Mother would be just furious if she knew I was saying "hell," but it's the only way to describe it. Standing underneath that glaring sun was enough to make me think I was burning in a real fire. It was so hot. It was unbearable.

After we made it to the hospital, we had to stand in line for hours and hours and hours. I hate standing in line. There is nothing to do in line and nowhere to go, because if you leave the line, you lose your place. It is just standing and waiting with nothing to do. It is the most boring thing you could do.

***

I watched the people come out of the hospital after getting tested, most of them were in tears or at least looking very serious, as if they wouldn't laugh even if they heard a joke. These people had just been told that they were not immune, and that if a cure did not come soon, they would die.

As I got closer and closer to the end of the line, I became more and more afraid. I didn't want to know if I was infected, or not. I wanted to keep living as I was, just living. To know for certain that I was dying was to die. That's the way I looked at it.

My mother got tested before I did. I went into the testing room when she came out. Mother was not crying when she came out, but she was not smiling either. She could have been in shock from having learned that she was immune, or she could have been in shock from learning that the virus would, indeed, kill her. I didn't have time to ask. A strict nurse was pushing me into the room and up onto the bench.

"Listen up," she said to me, lifting a big needle off a table. "We're going to take some blood out of your arm. It's part of our testing. Don't struggle or it will only hurt worse."

I didn't like the way she said that. "Hurt worse." That meant it was going to hurt.

The craziest thing happened then. You wouldn't believe me if I told you. What happened was this: just before the nurse could stick me with the needle, she clutched her chest and fell onto me.

It was the most horrible thing I have ever felt or seen. I wished Mother was there to cover my eyes that time. The nurse fell on top of me, and she was so heavy. She made me feel sick. Then the nurse slid to the floor and just lay there. I could see her eyes were open and not blinking, and her one arm was bent in a funny way. And I just had to look away. I couldn't look at her out of real fear. I tried to look at the ceiling and I screamed and screamed and screamed. It was the kind of screaming where I screamed until I ran out of air, took another breath, and then just kept right on screaming some more.

I couldn't understand why no one was coming in to see what had happened. Nobody opened the door or anything. Not even to check.

Now I realize that everyone outside must have thought I was screaming because of the needle.

When I looked at the nurse on the ground again, she looked like a sleeping squirrel. I put my hands over my own eyes, because I didn't think Mother would like me looking at the nurse. I kept my eyes closed and climbed off the bench and went to the door.

When I opened the door, mother was on the other side. She took me in her arms and scooped me up and carried me out of the hospital.

As she carried me, I peeked my eyes open a bit. I saw a lot of hospital workers rushing around with patients who needed to be checked. I realized then that every hospital worker who was working probably knew already that they had the Durmon virus. They had all already been checked, no doubt about it. Every nurse and doctor in that place knew they were going to die. They were working for their lives.

*Maybe this next one will be the one,* they were saying to themselves with every patient.

At first I was so frightened by seeing the nurse fall down and die right in front of me that I forgot I didn't get tested. I didn't remember that I hadn't been tested until I was back home in my bed, ready to fall asleep.

*Oh dear,* I thought in the darkness, *what should I do?* I decided that it could wait until morning because it was possible that I would die before then, and if I did, I wouldn't need to be tested; I would just need to be buried, like that squirrel.

*** 

If only I hadn't waited till morning, maybe things would be different. Maybe there would still be people.

# Chapter 15

In the morning we found out that most of the staff at the hospital had died sometime in the night, and that so had many of the people who had been waiting to be tested. The area around the hospital was blocked off because of the amount of corpses there were. This was announced on the radio. The radio also informed us that the chances of finding anyone with an immunity to the virus were slim to none, and that Maggie Millburn and the other scientists would be testing possible cures on any human subject who was willing to take them.

"What does that mean?" I asked mother.

"It means that they have made medicines that they believe might be cures. They will try a cure on a person to see if it works. They do not know what the cure will do, whether it will help, or make things worse. They just stir some ingredients up in the lab and feed them to somebody to see what happens, to see how the virus reacts. It's really quite dangerous. They have no clue how their 'cures' will affect the human body."

"You're very smart," I told mother, "You should be a scientist."

Mother laughed and took a sip of her tea because that's what she was drinking then.

"Mother?" I said.

"Yes?" she said back to me.

"Mother, when you got tested, did they tell you if you were immune or not?"

"Yes they did," said my mother.

"Were you immune?" I asked.

"Do you think I would be here if I was?"

I knew Mother must not have been immune, but I thought that maybe there was a chance that she was. Just a one in a million chance. That was all I really wanted.

"What about you?" Mother asked me.

"Oh," I said, looking at my foot because I didn't want to look Mother in the eye. I didn't want to tell Mother the truth about what happened yesterday because I knew it would worry her, but I had to tell her. I couldn't keep it a secret from her. "Mother, I didn't get tested."

"You didn't?"

"No, Mother, I didn't. The nurse died of the Durmon virus right in front of me. She never took my blood or did any tests or anything."

"Is that why you screamed?" Mother asked.

I gulped because I didn't want to cry, and then I said, "Yes."

"I'm so sorry, Maggie," Mother said, which made me want to cry even more. "I wish I had known."

"It's OK," I said. I was trying to be brave like Paul. Paul would never cry if he saw someone die. "But Mother," I said, "I didn't get tested. Isn't that bad?"

Mother thought for a moment and finally said, "Well, it doesn't matter. They've given up on finding anyone who is immune, so it's really no use getting you checked now. Better to just leave it be. But are you sure you're all right?"

Maybe if Mother hadn't said that, things would be different. Maybe if she had said, "You must get tested! It is your duty to the human race," I could have cured everybody.

It doesn't matter. I wasn't the only one who didn't get tested. Paula said in one of her letters that none of them had been tested because there were no doctors left in the whole state.

\*\*\*

It was very dangerous to travel at this time because drivers sometimes died of heartbreak in the middle of speeding down the highway, and they crashed. There were even some airplane pilots who died, causing their planes to spin out of control and hit the ground. The scientists issued an order that no airplanes could be used unless it was a real emergency.

\*\*\*

I went to Paul's house that evening, and he showed me the letter he got back from Paula. He was so pleased that Paula was still alive. The more he talked about Paula, the more I got a headache.

"She wrote a bit for you," he told me excitedly. "She's very smart to have thought of what she thought of. She told you a way to make Zola's story end differently every time! It's very clever. And she asked you to send her the story once you were finished, so she could read it."

"How thoughtful of her," was what I said.

Paul showed me the letter.

*Dear Paul,*

*Your picture is fantastic. I sleep with it tucked under my pillow, now, for luck. You are so handsome. I am blushing for saying it, but it is true and so I have to.*

*Tell Maggie that a good way to make a story end differently every time you read it is to stop writing it just before the end, so that everybody has to guess what the ending is for themselves. Then when two people who both read it talk about it with each other, they will both say how they think the story ends, and each will have to read it again, this time with the new idea. That's the best I can think of, because you can't just write thirty different endings and put them all at the end, because even then you can only read it again thirty times. And plus that would get so complicated.*

*I have started reading* The Orphanage on Palmer Street, *and I am about halfway through it. It is OK, but I don't like it too much. I think the writing is flat and monotonous, don't you? And sometimes it doesn't even use complete sentences. I can't make sense of it. I'm glad you like it though.*

*I was so relieved when I got your letter, Paul, that I fainted. I really fainted. A lot of people are dying out here, and it is so frightening. I hate this nasty virus. I hate it, I hate it, I hate it. Father says it is bad to hate anything, but I hate it.*

*My mother has gotten worse. She believes she can talk to the virus inside her heart. She claims that she and the virus have an understanding. She is always leaning forward and putting her hand over her mouth and whispering to her chest. She does this all the time.*

*Sometimes when she is upset with me, she will whisper something to the virus and I think she is talking about me. Why would she mention me to the virus? It is very strange. She acts more normal in the evening when Father is home, but when he leaves for work in the morning, she acts wild.*

*I have to go now,*

*Love,*

*Paula.*

"What's this?" I said. "Why doesn't she like your favorite book?"

Paul looked down at the ground in a shy way. "Well," he said, "I think she is much smarter than me, and maybe I didn't really understand, back when I read it, how good or bad the book was."

"That's hogwash," I said, meaning it was ridiculous. I had heard my mother say hogwash and I thought it sounded so funny so I said it sometimes.

"It doesn't matter," said Paul. "It isn't really my favorite book, anyway. I just like it, is all. Now quiet while I write her back."

"Why do you have to write her back all the time?" I asked, all annoyed.

"Because she will worry if I don't," was his reply.

*Dear Paula,*

*I didn't say last time, but your photo is very beautiful. I will say it because you said mine was handsome, and the truth is yours is very beautiful too.*

"Why are you writing that now?" I screamed. I screamed it so loudly that I heard a dish clatter in the kitchen below. It was probably Paul's mother I had startled.

"What?" said Paul, looking at me shocked. "She told me I was handsome. I have to tell her something nice back. It's polite."

"No you don't," I said, trying to tear the paper away from him. "You can just leave it be. You don't have to say anything like that."

"Well, I want to," said Paul, holding onto the paper with all his might.

"Well, you really shouldn't," I said. "It's not polite. Girls don't want to be told they're beautiful, and besides, you've never told me I was beautiful anyway so why should you tell her? Shouldn't you tell your friends that they're beautiful, first? Isn't that more polite, anyway?"

"Paula is my friend," said Paul.

When he said that I let go of the paper and stepped back and just looked at him. My heart was hurting, and I got really scared that I was dying.

"Help," I whispered.

"Just shut up," said Paul.

My heart started to hurt worse then. "Help! Help!" I screamed, holding onto my chest.

Paul looked at me and said, "Don't play around like that."

Paul made me so angry when he said that, that I said, "I'm never coming back here again," and left.

I was serious about that when I said it, but I forgot all about it later.

# Chapter 16

*The Orphanage on Palmer Street* is a very interesting book. It is the kind of book that I like a lot. It is about a boy named Joey Badge. I think Joey is the boy from the cover. The way that the book starts is this: Joey's parents send him to an orphanage because they do not like him. Joey is not a bad kid, but he doesn't always listen.

One time when his parents told him to go to bed, Joey opened his window, climbed onto the roof, and stood on top of his house with his arms stretched out. When his mother found him like that, she asked what on earth he was doing.

"I am pretending to be Moses," he said, with his arms stretched out.

"You'll break your neck," his mother said.

Joey liked to do things that were dangerous sometimes. It's not that he liked danger, he just didn't think that what he was doing was all that dangerous.

Sometimes when it was time for bed, he would climb out of his window and go for a walk in the dark. He did this so that he could think.

Joey's parents really hated Joey. His father would beat his face if he was found out of bed at night, or if he was found sneaking a spoonful of sugar, or if he was found not doing his studies. I think this is why Paul liked this book so much. Maybe he could understand how Joey felt when his father was mean to him.

Well, Joey got sent to the orphanage where he met all these extraordinary other boys, and he instantly became friends with all of them. There was one boy who was nicknamed "Bug," because he wore big glasses, which made his eyes look like compound eyes. Every boy had their own nickname, which had something to do with them. Joey's best friend at the orphanage was a boy named Nick whose nickname was "Name." The boys in the book thought this was very clever. I think it is too.

Name and Joey, who's nickname the boys decided would be "Checker," because on his first day at the orphanage he was wearing a shirt with black and red squares on it, like a checkerboard, started to go out of the window of the orphanage at night to take walks and go on adventures together.

They went to the cemetery and pretended to be ghosts and tried to scare each other, which was fun until they got scared and had to run back. They went to the woods at the edge of town and threw rocks in a creek. One night they climbed onto the roof of the orphanage and pretended to be Moses and Aaron. Checker, or Joey, stood with his arms spread wide and imagined that God was splitting the Red Sea in half so the Israelites could walk through, and Name, or Nick, was pretending to be Aaron, guiding the people through.

"Go on," he whispered to the imaginary Israelites, "go on through, it is perfectly safe."

Joey and Nick eventually invited the other boys to join them on their adventures, because it was more fun with more boys.

They formed a gang, the boys did. It was just a play gang. It wasn't real. The members were Checker, Name, Bug, Ham, Toothy, and Frostbite. Frostbite was so named because when he was dropped off at the orphanage, it was the dead of winter and his fingers were blue. They were not blue anymore, but he was still called Frostbite.

Here is one of my favorite parts of the book. This part happens on their first night out as an official gang. They have shovels because they want to dig a tunnel, which they can use to go anywhere in the city without anyone finding them.

\*\*\*

Joey led the way with a shovel over his shoulder. The shovel was heavy, and it smelled like dirt. Joey didn't mind the smell of dirt as much as he minded the smell of flowers. Joey didn't like the smell of flowers, at all. His mother had always smelled like flowers, and it gave him a headache. She smelled like flowers especially on Sunday, so that was his least favorite day because that was the day he got the worst headache. Yes, Joey really did like the smell of dirt better than flowers.

"Where should we dig first?" wondered Name, who was behind Joey and carrying a spade.

"We should start at the candy shop on Topper Street," said Ham. "That should be our first tunnel. That way we can go direct from the orphanage to the candy shop whenever we want."

"Swell," said Frostbite.

"I like lollis and I like choklits," said Toothy with a big fat grin.

"Stuff it, all of you," said Joey, who had become the unofficial leader of the gang, "we'll dig our first tunnel out in the forest, that way no one will see us digging. We can make all the other branches of the tunnel to different places once the first tunnel is finished. That way we have an escape if we ever need one."

"Why should we need to escape for? If any bad guy ever bothers me, I'll throttle him," said Ham, swinging his shovel like a sword.

"Don't be such a dumb," said Bug, "if any bad guy comes after us, you'll be the first to run."

"I'm no coward," said Ham bravely.

"Prove it," said Name.

"You say how, and I'll do it," said Ham. "I don't fear a thing. I eat courage for breakfast."

"Oh shut up and let me think," said Name, thinking with a hand on his chin.

"All right," said Name, finally. "I got it."

"Let's hear it then," said Ham, ever eager.

"Say a bad word," was all that Name said.

All the boys in the whole troop stopped marching. Shovels and spades hit the stone street. Every youthful eye was turned on Ham, who gulped loudly.

"Go on," said Joey. "Do it, if you can."

"Can you?" Ham asked Joey.

"I can," said Joey.

"Then why don't you say one?"

"Because nobody dared me to," was Joey's wise reply.

The air around the boys was filled with intensity. Their little-boy hearts beat blood through their veins with incredible speed. Everyone was scared to blink and scared to listen. Would Ham say a bad word, or wouldn't he? They all really needed to know.

"Heck," said Ham, finally. "Heck and darn. Heck and darn and Gol'darn it all! Gol'darn it all to heck!"

The boys, at first, looked at Ham with pale faces, full of shock and terror. And then Bug started to giggle. When Bug giggled, Frostbite chuckled. When Frostbite chuckled, Name elbowed Frostbite for chuckling, and then started to laugh himself. Ham snorted. Toothy squealed. Joey bit his lip to try to keep from laughing.

It was no use, the boys all collapsed to the ground and rolled and laughed and laughed and laughed. They squealed and howled and sobbed with laughter.

"Gol'darn it all to heck!" cried Bug, with delight. His glasses were fogging up from all the laughing he was doing.

"And son of a gun too!" cried Ham, happy tears rolling down his cheeks.

"Stop that racket!" came a voice from a window.

"Let's scram," said Joey between laughs. He picked up his shovel and took off. The other boys followed him. When they got out to the woods, where nobody could hear them, they laughed some more and tried to get Ham to say more bad words.

"I don't think I know any more," said Ham pleasantly.

"Oh go on," said Bug. "Make up a few if you have to."

"All right," said Ham, "just let me think for a moment."

Ham sat down on a log and put his chin in his hands. He stared at a caterpillar and tried to invent something bad to say.

"I've got it," he finally announced.

The boys cheered happily, and Ham stood up on his log as if it were a stage.

"Punch an old woman," he said loudly. The boys were quiet when they heard this. They looked at each other with confusion.

"Yeah," said Frostbite, after he'd thought about it. "Yeah punch her right in her noggin!"

"And kick an old man!" said Bug, eagerly.

Well, this just made those boys laugh until they could barely breathe anymore. They fell and rolled in those woods slapping their knees and yelling with delight. They had such a fine time that they forgot all about their plan to dig tunnels. It wasn't until it was almost morning that they remembered.

"Say," said Joey, "It's almost time for breakfast! What will Miss Mandalew say when she comes to wake us up and finds us all missing?"

"What should we do, Checker?" asked Name.

"We can dig there in time, probably," said Bug.

"Right," agreed Joey.

The group began to dig and soon realized that digging took a lot longer than any of them thought it would.

\*\*\*

Anyway, so after they try to dig for a while, they realize it isn't going to work, and so they decide to run back, and they run as fast as they can. They dash through the market, knocking people over and bumping into carts all just to get back to the orphanage on time.

When they get back, Miss Mandalew is waiting for them and they all get into really big trouble. It's so funny.

The book is full of funny stuff like that. The boys are always going off and getting into trouble.

I don't think Mother would have liked me reading the book if she had known that it had bad words in it. You really shouldn't say bad words. I think it's OK to read them, as long as you never say them. That's what I think.

Do you know what else I think? I think, "Gol'darn it all to heck and son of a gun too."

# Chapter 17

My piano teacher was a loud woman who liked to talk. She was the kind of woman who made me feel shy. When I was with her for my piano lessons, I was very quiet, even though I can get really loud.

She did this thing with me sometimes where she would actually talk *for* me, so that I didn't even have to talk at all myself, which I didn't mind so much except that sometimes she would make me say what I wasn't really thinking, which annoyed me.

Like this one time my mother came to pick me up, and she asked me how I was doing at piano. "Oh," said my piano teacher all loudly and happily before I could answer, "she's learned so much since she started. She really is improving. She was just playing a song today, and she was doing such a lovely job, isn't that right, little Maggie?"

She always called me little Maggie which really drove me up a wall. Boy, I hated to be called little Maggie. I'm not that little you know. I'm tall for my age.

Anyway, before my teacher even gave me a chance to say yes or no to her question, she was already talking again. This is where she would talk for me.

"Look at her," my teacher said to my mother, "she's like, 'Ah crazy lady, leave me alone already. I want to go home.'" Then my teacher laughed a really loud singsongy laugh. "But really her progress is incredible. She has so much natural talent."

My mother nodded and laughed along with my teacher. She didn't see that my teacher was talking for me. I wish she had noticed that. It really drove me crazy the way nobody noticed that except me.

"Well," said my mother, "she'll see you again next Tuesday."

This never made sense to me, either. Mother was talking about me as if I wasn't even there. Why would anybody do that?

"I'm looking forward to it," said my teacher. "Are you looking forward to it, little Maggie?"

I folded my hands behind my back and looked at a potted plant on her porch. The plant was a little red flower. I had tried to sniff it before, and it didn't smell too good. It smelled like grass or something. I don't mind the smell of grass but it's bad on a flower.

"You're like, 'Of course I'm looking forward to it,'" said my teacher. But she was wrong. I wasn't looking forward to it at all. I just wanted to go home.

My teacher's name was Mrs. Polly, which I thought was a parrot's name. When I asked Mrs. Polly if her name was a parrot's name, she laughed her singsongy laugh. I thought she was laughing at me, so I felt embarrassed.

For all of Mrs. Polly's weird things, she was good at teaching the piano. I could play "Fox in the Forest," and "Roundabout Jig," and "Two-foot Hop Step." These were my favorite songs to play because they sounded so happy and pleasant.

I like happy songs. I like songs with words about love or romance or just something nice. I would listen to a song about a toad if it was nice enough. I don't have any problems with toads.

One time Paul and I found a toad. I wouldn't touch it because I didn't want warts, and Paul wouldn't touch it either. The toad looked nice though. It sat there and blinked in the mud, and I could swear it even smiled at us. I suggested to Paul that we should name it.

"What should we name it?" asked Paul.

"We should name it Beautiful," I said.

"Why Beautiful?" asked Paul. "It's a toad. It's not beautiful at all."

"Because," I said, "it's probably never been called beautiful in its life, and everybody deserves to be called beautiful at least once."

And that was how we named our toad Beautiful. Beautiful looked like the happiest toad in the world when we told him what his name was. He really did smile. It was as if he understood what we were telling him.

When we got bored of looking at Beautiful, Paul decided to poke him gently with a stick to see what happened.

Beautiful jumped forward the second he felt the stick, and it made me scream. Beautiful was an excellent jumper. He could bounce all the way to the moon, I think.

*** 

The only reason I wanted to play the piano, anyway, was because Paul said to me once that he thought the piano was nice sounding.

"Maggie," he said to me, "I think the piano is the nicest sounding thing." When he told me that, we were listening to a song being played on the piano. The song was called "Boff's Twelfth Sonata." Esther Boff was a famous pianist who had her picture in the newspaper once.

Esther Boff had a large nose and black hair. She sat at the piano with a really straight back. She didn't slouch at all. Mrs. Polly told me all the time not to slouch, but I couldn't help it. I like to slouch too much. I'm doing it right now.

These days nobody tells me not to slouch. Do you know? I would chop off my right arm for somebody to tell me to sit up straight. I would chop off my right arm to see Mrs. Polly again, even if she never let me say another word.

I am really lonely. It is really lonely when everybody is gone.

Are you wondering where everybody is? I will tell you. I will try to tell you everything that happened. There's still some more things that happened before I got left all alone.

I'll say this: If you can help it, try to be with someone. You'll feel better. And if you've got to be alone, be alone, bravely, like me.

\*\*\*

I think if you put your mind to it you can be brave enough to do almost anything.

\*\*\*

I wish that I lived underwater inside a volcano surrounded by weird fishes. I wish I had gills instead of a nose. I wish that my story could end differently every time.

\*\*\*

Mrs. Polly, my piano teacher, had pale blond hair. Her body was shaped like a pear. She was like a really squishy rotten pear who laughed a singsongy laugh. She died of heartbreak. I think maybe the reason I don't die of heartbreak is because my heart is already broken. Maybe there's nothing left of my heart for the virus to eat.

# Chapter 18

Paul's father went crazy. That's what happened to him. I can't keep quiet about this for a second more. I've got to tell you how it happened. It's a mixture of scary and funny.

So Paul's father worked at a big building, according to Paul, and he sold insurance to people. Paul's father was obsessed with selling insurance to people. He was totally into it. It was all he could do, practically.

Before the Durmon virus started killing people, Paul's father was doing really well at his job. He got a new promotion every day. He was making gobs of money, just loads of it. Paul's father probably made the most money in the world.

Well, once the virus started killing everybody, people stopped buying insurance. They used their money mainly for food, because food keeps you alive better than insurance does.

So as the Durmon virus progressed, Paul's father got more and more desperate. He was getting poorer and poorer every minute. I remember once, I went to Paul's house and he was just standing in front of the fireplace with his hand on the mantle. He was staring at the wall, and he wasn't moving at all.

Paul's mother carried a plate of mac and cheese to him because he hadn't eaten. "Here," she said, "you need to eat something."

"Oh please, Mrs. Wilks," he replied, looking at Paul's mother as if she was someone else, "won't you please consider buying some insurance today? You don't have to buy very much insurance. Just a little insurance will be fine. Don't you want to be partially insured? Wouldn't it be nice to be a little bit insured?"

After he said that, he looked back at the wall.

Paul's mother was not named Mrs. Wilks, so I think he was talking about someone else. Paul's mother was actually named Betty. Isn't that nice? Her name makes me think about baseball in the summer, which makes me think about cotton candy, because cotton candy is the only reason to go to baseball, anyway.

After that, Paul's mother scooped a bite of macaroni into Paul's father's mouth. He chewed without thinking and without moving.

That wasn't even the craziest thing Paul's father did. As time went by, he did stranger things than that. One time I went to the house, and Paul's father was there in a pair of shorts and a T-shirt. "Hello," he said to me cheerfully. It was strange because Paul's father was never nice or cheerful, and he especially never spoke to me.

"Hello, sir," I said. I was really itching to go upstairs to the attic, and so I was bouncing on my toes while he talked to me.

"Tell me," he said, "would you be interested in some insurance?"

"I don't think so," I said.

Paul's father burst into tears when I said that. He cried out loud like a baby. It was frightening, so I ran to the attic to get away, but I could still hear him crying. His tears had been so big. When I got to the attic, I started laughing. I think he could hear me laughing because his crying got even louder, and I heard Paul's mother go comfort him.

It really is a shame to lose your mind. I hope I never lose mine.

As for the craziest thing Paul's father did, this happened at around eight o'clock at night. I was actually just about to go home when in barged Paul's father. He grabbed me by my arm and threw me into a grandfather clock. It really hurt my arm, but I wasn't too upset because I knew he was crazy.

Paul's mother was really horrified when she saw, though. She screamed at me and Paul to run and hide in the bathroom and lock the door.

"Be quiet," said Paul's father. He was swinging and staggering around in the living room. He was wearing a suit, but it was trashed. It was really scary to watch him. Paul couldn't move out of fear.

"Please, Father," he said.

Paul's father didn't like to be pleaded with. It really made him crazy. He slapped Paul across the mouth, and Paul fell over. Paul's mother started screaming, then, and crying. The noise must have really bothered Paul's father. He started pulling out his own hair. He was really grabbing it and tugging it right off his head. His eyes were red too. He looked like what I imagine the devil looks like, scary and dumb.

I really think the devil is extremely dumb. You'd have to be very silly to try to fight against God. Yes, the devil must be a total idiot. That's why people do dumb things. It's because the devil gets inside their heads. The devil has definitely been in my head before, because sometimes I'm the dumbest person I know. I've done a lot of stupid things is what I mean. I'm not like some people who do stupid things but never admit to it. I know I've done stupid things.

One stupid thing I did was get jealous of Paula. It made me nasty. And nobody can like you when you're nasty, even if they'd like you all right otherwise.

When Paul's father slapped him, Paul passed out right there on the spot. I was scared but I didn't cry. I just felt cold and scared. Sometimes you don't cry. Sometimes you just feel cold and scared.

"Shut up!" Paul's father screamed. "Shut up! Shut up! Shut up!"

He started to knock over lamps and just about anything

else he could knock over, which just made Paul's mother cry even harder. When she wasn't feeding Paul's father macaroni, she was basically useless.

What I did was, I crawled over to Paul. I went behind the couch, so Paul's father wouldn't see me, and got down next to Paul and put my hand on his forehead. It felt a bit warm, which was probably good. His hair was messed up from being hit in the face, and so I smoothed it down. It didn't look perfect, but I didn't have Paul's comb so there was nothing I could do.

Paul's father didn't calm down.

"What's the matter?" Paul's mother tried to ask.

"This is just the cake," said Paul's father. "Ten years I give you. Ten years of hard and honest work, and then it's not so much as a week's notice. It's goodbye to you all. It's farewell and see you never again. It's all a loss! It's all a waste." Paul's father looked at Paul's mother. "You can live your full life," he said with a shaky voice, "trying to achieve something and really honestly working at it, but in the end it all just falls apart. I don't understand. I don't get it. I don't get *Life*. Life is a phony. Life is just one big, fat, fatal heartbreak! What's the point of working? What's the point of even moving? What's the point of loving? It's all loss. That's all it is. You lose things, and you lose things, and you lose even more things until you've lost everything there is to lose, and then you lose your own limbs, your own head, and your own heart gets taken over by some little bug that eats itself to death! I've really had it with Life, Betty. Life's a problem. Life's never been good to any of us, and someone really ought to put a stop to it. It's tormented everybody who's ever lived it. It's never cut anyone any slack. It's, it's, it's…"

"What is it?" asked Paul's mother. She really wanted to know what "it" was. I was trying to decide if I should hold Paul's hand or not. I was worried that he would suddenly wake up if I did and be really mad at me for holding it.

"I don't know what it is and I don't know how to stop it," said Paul's father. "It won't stop. It goes on and on and on. It's eternity. Eternity is just the amount of time that I've existed. Look at it! It goes on forever. I never see it end. It's just me, stuck in Life. I've existed forever. I am inside my own eternity getting pushed around by Life."

"What are you going to do?" asked Paul's mother.

"I've got to defeat it, don't you see?" said Paul's father. "I've got to stop Life before it breaks anyone else's heart. People are dying of heartbreak, and it's all Life's fault. There's the cause for you. Send that to Maggie Millburn. Send it to her! Call her right now! Tell her Life is the reason everyone is dying all the time!"

Paul's mother went to the phone, but she didn't call Maggie Millburn. She dialed for the police. The police took Paul's father away, and I never saw him again after that.

It was all silly, the things he was saying. Not all things fall apart. My pink bike still works fine. So there.

# Chapter 19

When Paul left, it was the last time I cried. It was his mother's idea to leave. She decided to take all of the money that Paul's father had left them and use it to get Paul and her to the lab where Maggie Millburn and the other scientists were testing cures on people. Her idea was to go there and volunteer Paul and herself to have cures tested on them, so that maybe they would live. When I think about it like that, it makes me happy because I'm sure they got there just in time, and that they got a cure before the place was shut down. I'm sure they're on their way back here now, happy and healthy. That's got to be it.

Paul didn't tell me that he was leaving because he didn't know he was. If he had known he was leaving, he would have told me so that I could come and say goodbye.

I was riding my bike to his house, and sweating, as usual. And when I got to his driveway, I saw his car pulling out of it. He was in the back seat, and he was just screaming. I've never seen Paul scream like that. He was really livid. He was angry. When he saw me out of the back window of the car, he climbed right up to the window and started pounding on it.

"Paul!" I screamed, and I started to chase after the car on my bike. Mother always told me to ride only on the sidewalk and never on the actual road, but I ignored her this time. "Paul!" I screamed, chasing after the car as fast as I could, pedaling like crazy, but it kept speeding up. My feet were pedaling so fast that my legs were hurting from the effort, really hurting. They felt as if they were breaking, I was moving them so fast.

This is where I wish I could change the story. I wish I could say that the car stopped. If I could say that the car stopped, I would say it like this:

The car came to a stop, and Paul leaped out of it. He ran to me and took my hand. "I can't speak to you for very long," he said, "because Mother wants us to go, quickly. We can't waste any time. See, we're going to get a cure from Maggie Millburn. If it works, I'll be sure to bring one back to you, so just stay alive till then, OK?"

"OK," I said, trying my hardest to stay alive so that I wouldn't disappoint Paul. "What if I never see you again?" I asked, and the effort of saying it made me choke up a bit.

"But you will," said Paul. "We're coming right back. Right after we get cured. I promise."

"Say something to me," I said. "Say something to me that you would only say if it was the last time you were ever going to see me."

"All right," said Paul, still holding my hand. He got a bit shy, but he still said this, "Maggie, you are my best friend, and you are my favorite person to see." Paul paused to think, "Thank you for always coming to visit me in the attic. Thank you for playing pirates with me. I like you a lot. I like you more than I can say." Paul squeezed my hand tightly, which I think was him trying to say how much he liked me. Then he said, "I think when I get back, we should stay in my attic forever and never leave, and that we should have children of our own who can play with us in the attic, and we can read your stories about Zola to them at night before they sleep, so they can dream about volcanoes at the bottom of the ocean and weird fishes."

"All right," I said quietly, and my stomach started to hurt a bit but in a good way, "now I'll say something to you." I cleared my throat because I didn't want to sound emotional. "Paul," I said, "you're not allowed to like any girl but me. That's a rule, you can't break it. I like you a lot. No actually, I think I love you. I think I love you like they do in the movies, Paul. You know? I think I love you in the way that I want to hug and kiss you when you come home. OK? You must let me hug and kiss you the next time I see you. That's another rule. You can't break that one either. If you break that rule, I'll kick you. We should have four children, that way each of them has a friend. But we should get married first and go on a honeymoon to Paris. We should teach our children French because it is a beautiful language. I heard it in a movie once. They say hello by going 'bonjour.' Isn't that nice? And we'll all have a wonderful time in your attic, saying 'bonjour' to each other for the rest of our lives. That's all, OK?"

"OK," said Paul. "I've got to go now."

"Do you have your comb?" I asked.

Paul nodded.

"Goodbye, Paul," I said.

"I'll come right back," said Paul, and he turned and walked back toward the car. "And I won't break any of your rules," he said over his shoulder, "I promise you that."

Paul got back in his car and waved at me through the back window until he disappeared in the distance.

***

That is how the story ought to go, don't you think?

Well, what actually happened is, I chased after Paul on my bike, and he kept pounding on the window. He was trying to say goodbye to me. He wanted to talk to me. I know he did. I could see him screaming my name.

"Maggie!" he was screaming.

"Paul!" I was screaming.

"Maggie, we're leaving!" he screamed. "I didn't know!"

I pedaled my bike as hard as I could. Tears blurred my vision because I was crying as I was screaming. The car just kept getting farther and farther away. Paul's mother would not stop.

They started to drive up a hill, and that is where I lost it. I couldn't pedal anymore. It was too hard to pedal up the hill. I got off the bike and pushed it up the hill, running with my tired legs.

When I got to the top of the hill the car was gone, completely.

"Paul," I said. "Where did you go?"

\*\*\*

I rode my bike back slowly, on the sidewalk. I was still crying when I got back to Paul's house. I went up to the door and saw a note on it.

"If anyone wonders where we are," said the note, "we have gone to Maggie Millburn's lab to be tested on, in hopes of finding a cure." It was signed by Paul's mother.

I do not know why Paul's mother didn't stop. I cannot figure it out. All I wanted to do was to say goodbye to Paul. That was all. Maybe it was because I spilled ice cream on her floor. That's probably why.

\*\*\*

I sat on Paul's porch until I was done crying. That was the last time I ever cried.

# Chapter 20

My mother started going to work again. She worked at a store that sold food and other necessities. I told her I didn't want her to work, but she said she had to if I wanted to eat. And I did want to eat.

For work, Mother had to leave early in the morning and come back in the evening. When she was gone, I stayed at home and either read *The Orphanage on Palmer Street* or wrote about Zola. There wasn't anything else to do besides that.

I don't want to spoil how *The Orphanage on Palmer Street* ends because then you won't want to read it, so I'll just say that it was really great.

After Joey and the gang got in trouble for being out after bedtime, a new woman came to the orphanage to take care of them. This new woman was called Mrs. Stonewall. She was fat and ugly and angry and mean. She made all these strict rules so that the boys could never escape or have any fun. Every morning they had to wake up at exactly five o'clock. They had fifteen minutes to eat cold porridge for breakfast, and then they worked in the garden until seven. At seven they went inside and studied schoolbooks until

1:30 p.m., when they had a lunch of cold vegetables and baked beans. After that they were locked in their bedrooms and forced to take an afternoon nap. If she heard them running around or anything, they would get beat with a paddle. After the afternoon nap, the boys were forced to scrub the orphanage from top to bottom. Then they were given a cold dinner of ham and water and sent to bed.

The boys hated Mrs. Stonewall and for good reason. She was a monster and a bully. I couldn't even stand the bits where she stomped in and yelled and beat the poor orphans, who were unloved enough already. Fortunately Joey stayed in good spirits and kept the other boys cheerful too. He would make faces when Mrs. Stonewall wasn't looking and mouth the word "heck" at anybody who seemed ready to give up, which always made them smile. Joey was a real hero.

Finally the boys had had enough, and so they made a plan to get Mrs. Stonewall kicked out of the house so that it would be just them. They could take care of themselves just fine, after all.

This part is another really good part of the book. It is them making their plan.

*** 

Joey crept as quietly as he could to the side of Name's bed. Name was awake and looking at the doorway with frightened eyes. He imagined that Mrs. Stonewall was listening just outside the door for the slightest sound. She had such strong ears.

"All right," whispered Joey. "I've been working on a plan, and I think I've got it."

"You spit in my eye," whispered Name, rubbing his eye.

"Sorry," whispered Joey.

"Really it's all right," whispered Name.

"Well, listen," whispered Joey, "we'll need to gather all the boys together so I can explain it to everybody."

"There now," whispered Name. "You've spit in my eye again."

"That one wasn't my fault," whispered Joey. "You moved your head into it."

"Sorry," whispered Name.

"It's no problem, honestly," whispered Joey. "Now you know how next weekend Mrs. Stonewall is taking us on an outing?"

"Yes," whispered Name.

"Well," whispered Joey, "she can't act like a tyrant in public or the people will suspect something foul is up. She'll probably let us run about in the park. When she does that, I'll be able to tell everyone my plan."

"Shhh," hissed Name.

Joey shut up and listened. There was the softest and most dreadful creaking coming from just outside the door to their room. Joey froze as stiff as an ice cube and held his breath.

Name shivered as if he was lying in a bed located at the north pole and not an orphanage on Palmer Street.

The creaking grew louder and then stopped. The quiet after the creaking stopped was so quiet that you could hear the dust settling. It sounded like a million specks gently touching the ground all at once.

Joey watched the doorknob without blinking. He was just waiting for it to turn and for Mrs. Stonewall to storm in and kill him. He knew she would kill him if she found him out of bed. She had promised all of them that she would.

"If I find any one o' ya's is up after bedtime," she had said on the day she came to the orphanage on Palmer Street, "I'll slit yar throat."

Joey slowly brought his hand up and wrapped it over his throat.

Suddenly the creaking sound started again and moved away from the door. Joey heaved a quiet sigh of relief.

"That was close," he whispered.

"You tell us your plan at the outing," whispered Name, "you just tell us boys your plan then."

Well, time passed slowly as it does when one is expecting something, but finally the day of the outing came. The boys were all dressed in sharp navy-blue uniforms, bandanas, and caps.

Mrs. Stonewall marched past them and gave them a list of rules, which they were to follow while out in public.

"No running," she said, "no laughing, no talking, no smiling, no coughing, no sneezing, no falling over, no squealing, no skipping, no nose-picking, no emissions of gas, no eating, no drinking, and no engaging in any inappropriate behavior. If you find yourself in a situation where you are wondering if what you are doing is against the rules, it is best to just not do it. If any rule is broken, the guilty boy shall be spanked thirty times with the paddle. Do I make myself clear?"

"Yes, Mrs. Stonewall," said the boys in unison.

The company left the orphanage and marched to the park in a perfect line.

Once they were there, it was just as Joey suspected. Mrs. Stonewall told them they could play in the meadow as long as they didn't dirty their clothes.

"All right, fellas, follow me," said Joey, taking the lead.

The boys ran out of hearing distance of nasty Mrs. Stonewall and began to plot. "Here's my bright idea," said Joey. "Mrs. Stonewall is a classic pig, right? She's the nastiest broad any of us have ever had the misfortune of laying our eyes on. Well, ugly people are usually the smartest, so my guess is she's about five steps ahead of us right now and knows everything we're saying."

"She knows that much?" said Bug, his eyes wide.

"Yeah," said Joey, "I'm telling you, the ugly people are always the smartest."

"If that's so, then how do you know so much?" asked Bug.

"Well, just look at him," said Frostbite, referring to Joey. "He's ugly as an apple." Everybody laughed about what Frostbite had said and then Joey went on.

"All right, so look, whatever plan we come up with, Mrs. Stonewall will be prepared for it because she's so intelligent. If she's five steps ahead of us, then what we have to do to outsmart her is make a plan where we skip the first five steps. Right?"

"That's a pretty good plan," said Name.

"There's just one problem with it," said Ham.

"What's that?" asked Joey.

"If Mrs. Stonewall is so smart, she probably knows that we'd make a plan like that. Don't you think?"

Joey hadn't thought of that. He sat down on the grass and crossed his legs. *How on earth do you outsmart someone who is as smart as Mrs. Stonewall?* he wondered.

"Hello boys," said a voice.

Joey looked up and saw that a girl had come up to them. The girl had long blond hair, which was nicely curled.

"Hello," said Joey, "and what do you want."

"I'm looking for anyone who wants to play Meadowball."

"What's Meadowball?" asked Toothy.

"Haven't you played it before?" asked the girl. "It's a marvelous game you play in the meadow. You split into two teams and one person takes a stick and the other person takes a ball, and the person with the stick hits the ball away while everyone else on his team runs around frantically trying to pick ten daisies apiece. The other team chases down the ball and they have to try to tag everyone before they all pick ten daisies, but they can only tag them if they have the ball in hand, so they have to toss it around while they chase the other team. Once you're tagged, you can't do anything but bounce up and down until someone on your team tags you with the stick, which unfreezes you, then you take the stick and give your daisies to the fellow who unfroze you, and you have to go free one of your other teammates. The team with the ball can stop the fellow with the stick if they tag him, and the only way for the daisy-pickers to unfreeze the fellow with the stick is if they all drop three of their daisies, which they aren't allowed to pick up again. The team with the stick gets a point if they all get ten daisies, and the team with the ball gets a point if they tag everyone. Isn't that loads of fun?"

"Sure it is," said Joey, "but what's your name, anyway?"

"I'm called Lily," said the blond girl.

"Wow," said Joey.

The boys all introduced themselves to Lily, giving her their real names and then their nicknames. She thought they were very funny, but she still liked them.

They played Meadowball for a while and when they were all exhausted from running and laughing and arguing, which is how children play sports, they all plopped down on the grass.

"Do you know something, boys?" said Joey.

"What's that?" asked Toothy.

"I've got an idea for how we could defeat nasty ol' Mrs. Stonewall."

"Mrs. Stonewall?" said Lily.

"Yes," said Joey, "she's the cow who looks after us. She's a tyrant, isn't she boys?"

"Here, here," said the boys.

"Well, anyway," said Joey to Lily, "I've got this idea for stopping her. But I'll need your help to do it."

\*\*\*

That was the part of the book where the boys met Lily. She becomes a major part of the story as you keep reading.

A funny thing about reading that I think about now is I imagine all the books at the library with nobody to read them, and I imagine all the people who spent so much time writing those books so that people could read them. All the people who read all those books are gone now, so what was the point? When I think something like this, I always worry that I'm going crazy like Paul's father, so I make up a point.

The reason all those people wrote those books, even though there's nobody to read them anymore, is because they just had to.

***

*The Orphanage on Palmer Street* has a really good ending, so I'm happy I read it.

***

The day that I finished reading it was the same day that my mother never came home from work ever again.

# Chapter 21

This is something that happened before Paul left. Before Paul left, I went over to his house one night, and we went up to the attic. Paul wasn't in a very playful mood that night because he was missing his father. I didn't really miss his father, but Paul did. Paul just wanted to read *The Flight of the Nightingale* that night, so I just sat and watched him read it.

He was sitting on a box by the little window, reading. It was dark outside, but the moon was big and it shone into the room and made everything glow. Paul had a little flashlight, which he held up by his face, and shined on the page he was reading.

I was lying on the floor looking up at Paul. He looked focused. I was happy to just be there in the room with him. It was pleasant.

Paul had sent a letter to Paula earlier that day, which I didn't look at. I hadn't been paying attention to those letters anymore because they always made me angry when I saw them. I just ignored them now.

Finally Paul said to me, "Why are you still here?"

"Because I like it up here in the attic with you," I said.

"Is that all?" he asked.

"Of course," I said.

"Would you like me to read to you?" he asked.

"If it isn't too much trouble," I said sleepily, because it was dark out.

"All right," said Paul, "this story is about a pilot during World War II who flies an attack plane called *The Nightingale*. I'm on chapter seven so I'll just start there. Will that be all right?"

"Sure," I said.

Paul cleared his throat and began to read.

\*\*\*

Chip Dodger spun the plane upside down and then did a nosedive. The Japanese were on his tail and firing their guns at him. The guns went, *ratta-ratta, tatta-tatta.* Chip was very frightened. It was dark outside and very foggy, so he couldn't see anything. He had to rely on the gauges in the plane to not crash into the ground.

At the last second, he pulled up and spun his plane in a loop. The Japanese fighter jets did not give up pursuit. They stayed right on his tail. "Blast," said Chip as he listened to the ratta-tatta of the enemy guns. Chip thought back on his training about evasive maneuvers, then he remembered what his mother had told him the day he was shipped off to war. "Don't get shot by anybody," she had said to Chip on the dock while the crowds bustled past to board the large ship.

Chip remembered Duke, the dog he had owned when he was very young. *Duke would know what to do,* thought Chip. *Duke was a good dog.*

Chip spun the plane in a corkscrew maneuver until he was dizzy. Then he flew straight up until the engines were about to stall. He pulled back further, tipped over, and flew back down toward the Japanese planes.

He fired his own guns, which went, *chugga-chugga, gugga-gugga.* Chip hated the sound of guns. They were so loud and unpleasant. He hit one of the enemy planes and its wing blew up. The other enemy plane shot bullets, which hit *The Nightingale's* engine. The engine sputtered and then turned off completely. Chip was falling out of the sky in a tube of metal. It hurt his stomach to fall from so high up.

Chip unbuckled and tried to open the latch on the glass covering, so that he could jump out, but it was jammed stuck. "Come on," said Chip, punching the latch.

The plane was falling closer and closer to the ground, and if Chip didn't jump out soon, he would not have time to pull his chute. He would simply crash into the ground and die. Chip removed his pistol from his holster and aimed it at the glass. He fired a bullet and it shattered the glass. Chip pushed the leftover shards of glass out of the way and leaped from the falling plane. He tugged the string to release his chute, and for a long time it felt as if nothing had happened. He watched as the ground got closer and closer and he couldn't do anything about it. He was helpless. All he could do was fall.

Suddenly he felt as if a giant hand had caught him in midair and slowed his fall. He thought at first that it was the hand of God. Then he thought it was his dog, Duke. Then he realized it was only his parachute.

When Chip landed, he took off his parachute and folded it up. He had to hide it somewhere in case the Japanese Army investigated the crash. They must not know that he had survived. He carried the parachute into some nearby woods and hid it inside a hollow tree. He then began to look for help. Chip had to be very careful because he was in enemy territory. Nobody could be trusted.

As Chip walked through the woods, he came across a little house. He approached the house cautiously. It was a stupid thing to do, but he needed to steal some food if he was going to survive. When he got to the back door, he heard a noise behind him. He spun around, aiming his pistol, and saw that behind him was a young Japanese woman with a stack of wood in her arms. The woman looked at Chip with wide wet eyes. She shivered. She was quite beautiful too.

"It's all right," said Chip, "I won't hurt you." Chip put his pistol on the ground and kicked it away from himself so that the woman would not be frightened. She just stared at him with her big, wet eyes and would not look away.

"Don't worry," said Chip, and pointing to himself, he said, "friend."

The woman still did not move.

"Here, let me help you," said Chip, taking a step forward and extending his arms. The woman dropped the wood she was holding and took several steps back. She was wearing a simple nightgown. She was simply beautiful. Chip walked forward and picked up the wood that she had dropped.

"Where do you want this?" he asked.

The woman said nothing.

Chip began to walk toward the little house, but the woman stopped him. She ran up behind him and grabbed him by the arm. "What is it?" said Chip.

The woman spoke to Chip in Japanese, which he did not understand, and gestured at the house.

"I'm sorry," said Chip, "I'm very sorry, but I don't have a clue what you're saying."

The Japanese woman looked at Chip and said in Japanese, "I'm sorry, I'm very sorry, but I don't have a clue what you are saying."

Chip walked toward the door again, and the woman ran and stood in front of it.

"What is the problem?" asked Chip.

The woman tried to explain in her language that her mother and her brother were inside, and that her brother despised Americans because they were against each other in the war.

"If he sees you," she said in Japanese, "he will try to kill you."

Chip didn't understand, and so she made him set down the wood by the door. She took him by the hand and led him away from the house. She led him down a dirt path toward an old brown barn. She took him up to the hayloft and held up both her hands. She spread her palms and shook them. "Stay here," she was saying with her palms.

Chip pointed at the hay. "You want me to stay here?"

The woman nodded her head.

Chip climbed into the hay and crawled to the far back corner. The woman shoved hay over him, so that he couldn't be seen.

"I will keep you safe," she whispered in her language, but Chip didn't understand a word of it.

The woman left and Chip began to wonder if the woman was protecting him, or if she was running to fetch soldiers. *Ahh well,* thought Chip, *it can't make much difference now. I have no choice but to stay here.* And so that is what he did.

The woman ran back to her house and picked up the gun that Chip had left there and carried it inside. She hid it in her room, in her drawer of clothes. She then went into the kitchen and said hello to her mother and her brother.

"Where is the wood?" asked her mother.

"I'm sorry," said the woman. "I will go and get it."

"We need the wood," said her mother. "What have you been doing?"

"I was distracted," said the woman, "by how nice it was outside. I am sorry. I will get the wood now."

"Do not delay another second," said her mother.

The woman brought in the wood and dinner was cooked and eaten. After the woman's mother and brother had gone to bed, she snuck out to the barn with a bit of food for Chip.

"Here," she said, in her language to him.

"Gee," said Chip, taking the bread and the bowl of rice, "this is great."

He ate the food quickly, and he didn't leave a scrap of it in the bowl.

"Thank you," he said.

The woman did not look as if she understood him, and so Chip patted her arm to say thanks. She smiled just a tiny little bit, and then she left and Chip fell asleep.

\*\*\*

Paul stopped reading out loud there. After a while I said, "Paul?"

"Yes?" he said.

"That's a pretty good story," I said.

"It is interesting," was Paul's reply.

"I like to listen to you read," I told him. And then I asked, "What do you suppose the Japanese woman's name is?"

"It says that her name is Aiko in the next chapter," he answered.

"Yes," I said, "but what do you suppose her name is?"

"I suppose," said Paul, "that it could be Mitsuki."

"Why that?"

"Because," said Paul, "that is a nice name too."

# Chapter 22

For the first few weeks, when I was all by myself, it was really terrible. I was scared all the time. And Paul wasn't there to visit, so I couldn't even leave the house. At night it was the worst because I could hear all these strange noises in the house that I'd never heard before. I would hear clatters and creaks and moans and groans and just the most awful noises. It was so scary that I couldn't even sleep.

My first night alone was the night that mother never came back from work. I didn't notice she wasn't coming home at first because I was so into reading *The Orphanage on Palmer Street*. When I finished the book, it was dark out and I went down to the living room and said, "Mother, I'm hungry."

There was no reply. I wasn't worried just yet, though. I figured she hadn't heard me.

"Mother!" I said. "Could you please make me a snack?"

There was still no reply.

I went outside to look, but the car was not parked in the driveway.

*Where could she be?* I wondered. That was when I got it, the cold feeling. I felt something awful, like an icicle, pierce me in the chest. I was thinking that maybe the unthinkable had happened. Maybe, Mother wouldn't come home because... but I couldn't say because why. I wouldn't.

I wondered what could have kept her at work. Maybe, it was really busy and they needed her to work late. That was a possibility. Maybe, she'd been kidnapped. That was a possibility too. If so, I would only have to wait until she escaped and came home. Maybe, she had been picked up by a helicopter and flown to Maggie Millburn's lab to get the cure. That must have been it.

I'm sure Mother fought like mad when the helicopter picked her up.

"I have a daughter at home," she probably screamed, struggling against the people who dragged her on board.

"You must receive the cure," the pilot probably said. "It's very important that you do not die."

When I was first left alone, I was sure that this was what happened. Since so much time has passed, I have become less sure. I really hope Mother is all right wherever she is.

When I tried to go to sleep that first night without Mother, I couldn't sleep a wink. First of all, Mother always came into my room to wish me goodnight. So for about an hour, I sat in my bed and watched the door to see if she would come in to wish me goodnight. She didn't. I don't know what I was thinking. How could she have wished me goodnight? She was on a helicopter on her way to a lab. I was just being silly.

When I finally rolled over and turned off my lamp, it got about ten times darker than it usually does. I blinked as fast as I could to get my eyes used to the dark, but I couldn't see anything. I even tried putting my hand directly in front of my face, but I couldn't see it.

Then, in that awful dark, I thought I could hear the sound of someone breathing. It was an awful breathing sound. I thought perhaps the devil himself was in my room with me, and that it was him breathing.

"Mother?" I whispered. "Paul, is that you?"

The breathing got more and more frantic, and I started to shake. I couldn't move I was so scared. Finally I just had to grit my teeth and turn on the light. When I pulled the chain on my lamp, and the room lit up, there was no one but me in it. I checked in the closet and I checked under my bed and even in my toy box. There was nobody there but me.

I rooted through my toy box until I found my pop gun. I loaded it with the cork and climbed back into bed. When I turned out the light, I could hear the breathing again. I popped the gun blindly and held my breath. The breathing was gone. Whatever it was, I had got it.

After the breathing stopped, however, I could hear all the other awful noises. It sounded as if someone was walking around downstairs. It sounded as if the radio was on. It sounded as if someone was scratching the outside of my window.

It's terrible to be alone because the only thing that's with you is sounds and noises.

\*\*\*

In the morning I was really hungry because I hadn't even had dinner the night before. I had been too worried. I ate a big bowl of cereal with milk on it and then went into the living room and turned on the radio. I had my pop gun with me just in case.

On the radio I could hear the voice of Susan Cathalon. She sounded sad. "Folks," she was saying, "we intend to keep broadcasting for as long as possible, but every day it grows harder. Today I bring the sad news that Maggie Millburn has passed away. The research lab she ran has vowed to keep searching for cures without her and invites all willing people to come to the lab to be tested on. With each passing day, they come closer to finding a cure. They believe they have almost got it. Please, everyone, just hold on a few more weeks. They say that is all the time they need. The rate of people dying because of the virus has begun to rise again, and so we caution everyone: be careful, be safe, stay alive."

I turned off the radio because it was too sad to listen to. Maggie Millburn was gone. She had been killed by her own virus. Her child, as she called it, had killed her. It was very disturbing. I had never known of anybody with my name dying before.

*** 

At first I didn't miss Mother. I didn't miss her until a week or two later when it began to seem as if she would never come back again. I knew I ought to cry, but I just couldn't. No matter how hard I tried, I couldn't cry. I still haven't cried about Mother never coming home. I suppose I ought to, but I can't.

# Chapter 23

I didn't leave my house until I had eaten every scrap of food in it. When I had eaten all the food, I had to leave to get more. I didn't go to the store for food because that was too far away, anyway. Where I went was Paul's house.

The front door was locked and so was the back, but there was one window in the laundry room that didn't latch, and so I just pushed it open and climbed in. Paul's father was supposed to fix that window. Paul's mother was always reminding him that he had to fix it. Thank goodness he never did.

I went to the cellar in Paul's house, and I found a pail of ice cream. I ate the ice cream until I was all the way full, and then I went up to the attic and sat there all alone. I had my pop gun with me, but that was it.

After a while I got really bored. It is so hard to go a whole day without talking to anyone. I started to explore the attic. I opened every box and container and searched through everything. I really was a snoop.

After I had made a mess of the attic, I walked up to the little window and pressed my nose against it. When I looked down at the floor after looking out the window, I saw something. It was *The Flight of the Nightingale*. I picked it up and it opened where Paul's bookmark was, which was Chapter Eleven.

Paul must not have meant to have left it, since he hadn't finished it yet. I opened the book to just a random page and read a little bit.

*** 

Aiko came to Chip's hideout in the barn with a cup of hot tea. Chip was not feeling well at all. He was dreadfully sick.

"Here," said Aiko.

Chip took the tea and sipped it slowly, so he wouldn't burn his tongue. He started to cough but tried to muffle it by coughing into his arm.

"There, there," said Aiko, running her hand through Chip's curly brown hair. Aiko's hand was cool, and it felt so nice to Chip that he just closed his eyes and wished he could lie like that forever.

Chip was always lonely when Aiko wasn't there. It drove him crazy. Even though he couldn't understand a word she said, he loved Aiko with all his heart and soul. He would brighten up every time he saw her. The best medicine for Chip was simply to see Aiko's face. Each hour that she was not there seemed to be ten years long.

Chip had no news from the outside world. He had no idea what had become of the war. The only person he saw was Aiko. She was his life. He was very thankful for her.

While the faces of everyone else he knew faded into nothing in his memories, Aiko's face remained clear. It kept him from going insane. If it hadn't been for Aiko, he surely would have gone insane.

***

That was what it said.

***

Chip was really lucky to have Aiko. I am not like Chip. I don't have anybody. For a while Paula was the person who kept me sane, but I even lost her when the mailman stopped coming.

I did eventually take that book out of the attic and read the whole thing. I basically read it because I wanted to find out if Chip and Aiko would get married and kiss. That is a good way for a story to end. I won't give away the ending too much, but I'll say that I really liked it. It had a very nice ending.

For a while when I was reading it, I was worried that it wouldn't end well, at all. A lot of stuff went wrong after Chip got better from being sick. He was found by Aiko's brother, and he had to go out on the run. The whole time he was running, he was being chased by Aiko's brother and some other soldiers from the village. Chip was only able to keep running because he kept thinking about Aiko.

While Chip was off running from the soldiers, Aiko was trying to get her brother to let Chip live. When Aiko's brother realized that she had known Chip was in the barn the whole time and had been feeding him, he got really mad at her. He was about to kill her for betraying their country, but Aiko escaped.

What she did was, she ran into her room and took Chip's pistol out of her drawer. "If you wish to kill me because I helped a person in need, then you are a monster," she told him while she pointed the gun at him. I thought that the line she said there was a very cool line. I wish I could say something cool like that.

Anyway, she ran away from home, hoping to find Chip. When she ran away, the brother was so angry that he put up signs in all the nearby towns calling her a traitor and demanding that, if anybody found her, they turn her in. Chip was sneaking around in a town one night looking for food, when he saw one of these signs and recognized her picture, which was on the sign. He realized she was in trouble, and he got very worried about her.

Well, a bunch of stuff happened. Chip basically found out that she had been arrested, and he went to rescue her. He barged in like a real hero, and he broke her out of jail. The two escaped together, but then they were both on the run.

They were on the run for a while, going through the countryside. Aiko kept them fed because she knew what plants were edible in the wild. That was another way she saved Chip's life.

I thought for a long time that they wouldn't escape. I thought they would get caught and killed. I had to read it very fast because I was so worried. At every turn they kept getting nearly caught by the enemy. It was quite thrilling.

\*\*\*

And I am very happy with how it ended. I won't say any more than that.

\*\*\*

At first I would go to Paul's house in the daytime and go home to go to bed, but eventually I stopped doing that and just stayed at Paul's.

# Chapter 24

I can't believe it took me so long to think to check the mailbox. I guess when your mother is usually the one to do it, it doesn't seem that important to you, and so you don't think of it.

I actually don't think I ever would have checked it except that I happened to look out the window in the attic and saw the mailman drive by and drop off some letters.

*All right,* I thought, *I'll go see what's in the mail.*

I'll be honest, I was thinking that there was going to be a letter from Paula. That was what made me so curious to see what was there. I had stopped reading the letters Paul and Paula were sending each other, and so I had no clue what they had been talking about.

Sure enough, there was not one, but three letters in the mailbox from Paula. The first one was a normal letter, which was a response to the last letter Paul had sent. The second and third letters were both asking if Paul was all right.

This is what they all said in order:

First letter.

*Dear Paul,*

*I am so happy to hear that you like ballet. I have been practicing a lot, and I cannot wait to show you how much I have improved. I think it is a very elegant and artistic thing. That's what my teacher says. She says ballet is very elegant and artistic. My teacher talks with a funny voice, and so I can't always hear her. She said she comes from another country, and I think it's just a scream. You'll have to hear her sometime.*

*I think about Mother every day. I'm very sad about what happened to her. Whenever I think about her, I start to really miss her, and I get so sad that I just want to go to sleep and never wake up. Wouldn't that be wonderful? I wish I could be in a happy dream for the rest of my life.*

*You know those dreams where you can fly and lift buildings, where everyone is nice, and you don't feel any pain, at all? I would love to be trapped in a dream like that. It would feel safe and warm.*

*Your encyclopedias sound wonderful. I would love to look inside them at all the interesting information, and you're right, I'm sure they would help me find ideas for what sort of science experiments need done.*

*I wish I could visit you. Wouldn't that be weird? It would be strange, because we've spoken so much in letters that I feel as if I know you, but what if when I met you, you had a really funny voice or something? Wouldn't that be wild? You don't have a funny voice, do you? I asked my father if we could drive out to you, but he said that it wasn't safe.*

*It really is becoming a ghost town. I wish my father would agree to leave. Pretty soon it will be just the two of us.*

*To answer the question, you asked: Yes, I do. Very much.*
*Love,*
*Your Paula.*

Second letter.

*Dear Paul,*

*You haven't written me back in a timely manner, and I am worried. Please tell me you are all right. Are you all right, Paul? My father said that perhaps you had your heart broken, but I just absolutely refuse to believe it. You're a fighter, Paul. You would never die. Would you?*

*Please, if you get this, send me a response, so I know you are well.*

*Love,*
*Your Paula.*

Third letter.

*To the father or mother of Paul,*

*Hello, I am pen pals with your son, Paul. We have been writing back and forth over the summer. Now the letters have stopped coming. I am wondering, if you get this, whether you could tell me if Paul is all right? I am very worried about him. Mrs. Betty, my mother said that you and she were good friends when you were young. That was why she encouraged me to write to your son. She said that you and she used to do everything together. She said that Paul and I were named after the same person that you both knew growing up together. Please, just tell me if Paul is all right or not. If he's had his heart broken, please just say so.*

*I'm very sorry.*
*Sincerely,*
*Paula.*


The thing that drove me the most mad was that Paula was signing her letters with, "Your Paula." As if she belonged to Paul or something. It was ridiculous and unbelievable. I couldn't stand it. I also really wanted to know what Paul's question to her was. The one that she answered by saying, "Yes, I do. Very much."

That kind of answer could go with almost any question. It drove me mad. The third and final letter wasn't even addressed to Paul, but addressed to his mother and father. This was evident in the writing as well.

She was clearly very worried about Paul, and so I decided to set her mind at ease, and the best way I could think of to do that was to write back to her as Paul.

Now I think that was a silly thing to do because it made her think that Paul was fine. I mean, I'm sure Paul is fine, but the truth is I just don't know. I haven't seen Paul since the day he left. I haven't heard from him or anything.

It just seems silly now, is all.

This is what I wrote to her.

*Dear Paula,*

*Paul here. Sorry I haven't written in a while, I have been spending a lot of time with my friend, Maggie. She is funny because she makes me laugh all the time, and her book about Zola is very good. I am enjoying it. It might be my new favorite.*

*I'm sorry I worried you. I should have replied sooner. Please forgive me, if you would.*

*Yes the encyclopedias are extraordinary. Do you know, there is even a picture of a naked statue in one of them? It is so disturbing and yet fascinating at the same time.*

*The area around here is becoming more and more empty too, so you know. It's so quiet these days that you can hear everything, which seems to make the quiet things more loud. You know I never noticed how loud the quiet was before now. There is a faint fuzz noise that is always there, or else a ringing noise, or something like that. Sometimes I just sit there and listen to it to see if it is anything important. Perhaps it's a signal, you know?*

*I think living in a dream forever could be cool, but only if you could pick and choose who to have in the dream with you. I'd hate to be in a dream all by myself. That would be dull.*

*Sincerely,*

*Paul.*

I knew I should end the letter with "love," so that it would seem like Paul was writing, but I couldn't bring myself to do it.

I knew how to mail the letter off because I had watched Paul do it many times. I put the letter in an envelope, sealed it, wrote the address on the back, applied a stamp, put it in the mailbox, and put the flag up. That's all there was to it.

Now all I had to do was wait for a reply. I didn't know it then, but I would come to live for those replies from Paula.

# Chapter 25

Paula and I sent loads of letters to each other, and I never once told her it was me who was sending them. She thought I was Paul the whole time. It became like this whole mission of mine to sound like Paul in all the letters I sent her. After a while I even started to feel as if I was Paul. I would have conversations with myself where it was me and Paul talking.

"Paul," I would say to myself, "do you want to play pirates in the attic?"

"Sure thing, Maggie," I would say to myself, "just let me finish my chapter."

I think that I must have been on the verge of going crazy then. My only interaction with anyone was with Paula, and I didn't even get to interact with her as me.

We talked about all sorts of things in our letters. I told her things that I figured Paul would say, like how I had been studying oak leaves and so on, and she told me about the scary animals that lived in the desert like nasty poisonous snakes.

"The key to not getting bit by a poisonous snake," she wrote, "is to let them be. If you do not threaten them, they will not bite you. There was even a story of a man who fell down a hill and when he stopped rolling, he looked up and was face-to-face with a Striped Wompon, which is a very poisonous kind of snake.

"The snake looked the man in the eye, and the man whispered ever so softly that he was very sorry to have disturbed it. When the snake heard that, it slithered away. I think snakes are smart like that. Snakes are smarter than most people think."

Even though I didn't like Paula, I started to like her, just because there was no one else around to like. We got along very well in our letters, and if I ever felt like getting in an argument with her, she always managed to point out how silly the argument was in the next letter. I think maybe it was because she thought I was Paul that she tried to stop us from arguing.

I'll never forget the day I got this one letter from Paula, though. We had been sending letters for months when this one arrived. It was the last letter I ever got from her.

*Dear Paul,*

*My father went to the store to get some milk, and he has not come back for an entire day. I am very worried. I don't know what to do. I know the truth. The truth is that he must have died of heartbreak. There isn't any other explanation. It doesn't take an entire day to get a jug of milk. I know that much.*

*I don't know what I'm going to do now. I am all alone. I walked all up and down my whole street, knocking on every door I passed and nobody would answer. What am I supposed to eat? How shall I survive? I looked in the pantry and there are lots of foods in cans, but they will not last forever.*

*I have rationed the food, so that I don't eat all of it at once, but that's all I could think of to do. I'm sure you would know what to do in this situation. Maybe, I should try to hitchhike to the next town, but I'm not sure which way it is. I'm afraid that I'll starve to death. Please, if you could tell your mother or your father to come and get me, that would be just swell.*

*Love,*
*Your Paula.*

I did write a response to her letter. It was actually quite a good response. See, I had started to feel really bad about lying to Paula. I knew if Mother could see what I was doing, she would not approve, and so when she said that she was all alone, just like me, I decided to come clean, because I was the only person she had, and so I didn't think she would stop writing to me.

*Dear Paula,*
*I have a confession to make. I have not been honest with you. I am not Paul. I am Maggie. Paul is gone. He is not*

dead that I know of, but he is gone. He and his mother left to go to Maggie Millburn's lab to have cures tested on them. I'm sure he is perfectly fine, but he can't send you letters anymore.

I have been writing his letters for him for some time now.

As for your problem, I must say that I am in a similar situation. Everyone I know has vanished for one reason or another. What I have done is move from house to house, taking all of the food inside because there isn't anybody there to eat it anymore. There was one house where, when I broke the window to sneak in, the most awful rotten smell came out of it, and so I didn't go into that one. Every other house on my street is empty. If you check in the cellar for a freezer, you might even find some ice cream. Be sure you do that.

Please don't stop writing me because you found out I'm not Paul. You're the only person I can talk to.

Sincerely,

Maggie, not Paul.

And then I wrote this:

PS Please tell me why you answered Paul saying, "Yes, I do. Very much." I promise I won't be upset no matter what you were saying, I'm just too curious, is all.

***

I believe that it is important to be honest, even if being honest can hurt you. I told Paula the truth, which is what I should have done from the start. If I had done it from the start, I wouldn't have had to feel bad about lying to her in the first place. Isn't that silly? What's the point of lying if it just makes you feel bad? It's completely pointless.

I put the letter in the mailbox and put up the flag and went inside. The next day, the flag was still up. The day after that, the flag was still up. A week after that the flag was still up. The mailman had stopped coming. He never came and delivered my letter to Paula.

***

I never got another letter.

# Chapter 26

With Paula's letters gone, there was really nobody for me to talk to. What I did was, I started to write stories about me talking to people. That was all they were, just me talking with anyone I could think of. That way I could feel as if the stories were real, if I wanted to.

I wrote one story where my father came back from building houses in a foreign country. He took me out to Fast Food and bought me a big chocolate milkshake, the biggest size you could get. I drank the whole milkshake in two gulps, and so Father had to buy me a second.

I described the milkshake so deliciously in that story that I could almost taste it.

Father and I talked for a whole week about everything I could think of. He told me that he was very sorry that he had to leave Mother and I, and that if he could do it over again, he would stay with us and never leave the country. That was one of the nicest things anyone ever said to me.

I wrote one story where Paul came back, and he had the cure, so he was OK. The cure had turned his hair white, which was strange, but I was simply happy to see him again. We went on and on about how nice it was to see each other again and how we shouldn't ever get separated again.

Mother also came back with the cure, and she told me that she thought I had grown up a lot. I told her, "Welcome home. See? I was just fine without you."

I even wrote one where I talked to Paul's mother, and I apologized to her for spilling ice cream on her floor. She was very kind and forgave me almost instantly.

*** 

When the radio stopped broadcasting, it got quiet as the grave. After Paula stopped sending me letters, I was still able to listen to the radio. It wasn't like talking because you could only listen, but at least I could hear the sound of people's voices. That was very comforting.

I remember when it happened that there was no announcement that the radio was shutting down. It just stopped halfway through a broadcast. It cut right in the middle of a word.

The power went out not long after that. I couldn't turn on any lights in any of the houses on my whole street. That was bad, because the hot summer was over now, and it was the middle of winter.

I had so much trouble keeping warm without electricity. I had to learn how to make fires and wear a poofy coat everywhere, even inside. Luckily it was a warm winter, just like how the summer had been hot, but it was still shiveringly cold. I've decided I won't be here when next winter comes around.

***

Another thing about the power going out was everything that made noise in the whole world stopped making noise. I was the sole producer of noise. Sometimes I would go outside and stand in the middle of the street and scream as loud as I could just so that it wasn't so quiet. I can scream pretty loud too, you know.

I would stop screaming sometimes because I thought I heard someone screaming back. It was always just my echo though.

So I had a conversation with Abraham Lincoln where I told him that he was my favorite president. I had a conversation with Martin Luther King Jr. where I told him that he was really brave and smart. I had a conversation with Joey from *The Orphanage on Palmer Street*. I talked to anybody and everybody in my stories. It made the time pass, which was all I could do.

***

For a long time, I didn't write about Zola. I just couldn't do it. I didn't want to think about Zola living alone in a volcano at the bottom of the ocean. I couldn't imagine why she would like that. Imagine being all alone forever. How could anyone stand it?

Finally I wrote about her, and it was only because I had a great idea. I wrote that Zola found a rare ruby on the ocean floor. The ruby was fantastic, because it glowed this magical sort of glow, and when you looked at the way it glowed, you felt really happy. Zola knew that she couldn't keep this happiness to herself, because that would be selfish, and so she went to the surface. She swam up to a beach, which was crowded with people, and she walked out and showed everyone the ruby.

The people on the beach were mesmerized. The children giggled with glee when they saw it. It really made the kids so happy. Husbands and wives who saw the ruby couldn't help but to kiss each other when they saw it. They felt as happy as they had felt on the day that they first fell in love. It was wonderful.

Soon Zola was being flown to every part of the earth with her ruby. She met presidents and kings and queens of every country on earth and showed them her ruby, and they all smiled or laughed or cried happy tears. Zola was so happy to see everyone else feeling good.

The ruby had incredible powers. It made people forgive everyone who had wronged them, it made people apologize for the bad things they had done. It made people tell the truth, it made people be kind to each other, and it made everyone cheerful. People could have been this way from the start if they had just tried, but it took the magical ruby to make it so. Isn't that funny? I think that's a little funny.

After traveling with the ruby for a whole year, Zola was tired, and so she went to the beach to relax. While she was there, she remembered how she used to live in the ocean, and so she swam out a bit to see if she could still breathe underwater.

She dived down deep and tried to take a breath, and what do you know? She could breathe just fine. Her gills were still there. She swam deeper and deeper in the water. She swam so deep that it got pitch black, and she could only see by the glow of her ruby.

When she got this deep, she saw the strangest fish she had ever seen. There were some that looked like awful monsters with large teeth, there were some that were smooth and transparent. There were some that had tentacles, there were some that were long-legged crabs, and there were many, many others. Zola just kept swimming down. She wanted to see what was at the bottom of the earth. She was an explorer, after all. She needed to do some exploring.

The fish she met just got more and more wicked-looking the further down she got. There were fish you couldn't even imagine seeing in real life. Fish with horns, fish with three eyes, and fish with eight fins. There were fish down there with red and white spots, and fish that looked like gooey dogs. There were jellyfish too, that were shaped like cubes, and triangles, and other strange wild shapes. There were these fat dull fish that blinked slowly and swam slowly and were as solid as rocks when you touched them. There were narrow little fish that darted by you really fast. There were fish that had things that were almost like hands. There were fish with antennas on their heads and bellies. It was so mad.

When Zola went down farther, all the fish disappeared. Suddenly she just stopped seeing them. All that she could see was the darkness and the glow of her ruby. This darkness really scared Zola. It scared her a lot. She still would not stop. She had to see what was at the bottom. She had to know, and so she continued, alone, into the endless darkness.

\*\*\*

That was how I ended the book. I think it is the best way to make it so that it ends differently every time. That way you can wonder forever what happens to Zola. Did she find the bottom or did it go on forever? Who or what was at the bottom, if she found it? Did she ever return to the surface again? That's a good way to end a story. You've got to leave everyone wondering what on earth happens next. That way they can all come up with their own ending, and read it again with that ending, and they can change their ending too and read it all over again.

My favorite ending that I've thought of so far is one where when she gets to the bottom, she meets this group of humans who look just like regular humans but have gills like she does. She learns from them that she was their long-lost daughter who washed ashore when she was a baby. I like that ending because there is a big happy homecoming at the end, and you really don't expect it.

*** 

I hope real life ends like that. I hope there is a big happy homecoming at the end, and you really don't expect it.

# Chapter 27

Oh, how could I be so silly? In all this time, I forgot to mention how I met Paul. I should tell you that. Wouldn't you like to know?

Well, I met him at school. It was during recess, that I finally had the courage to speak to him. I had seen him in the classroom sitting in the back, leaning over his books with really wide eyes, and sometimes at lunch I would see him at the next table down, maybe combing his hair with his comb or else eating.

I was always shy when talking to new kids that I didn't normally talk to. I would hardly say a word when I met a new kid. Then suddenly, and I could never pinpoint exactly when this happened, but it seemed as if me and the new kid were talking and playing as if we had always been the best of friends.

Well, at recess I was standing by the swings waiting for some kid to hop off one of them. The only way you could get a shot at the swings at recess was to stand and wait for some kid to hop off one of them. The swings were the most popular part of recess, so you were lucky if you got a chance. Every kid wanted to ride them.

I was just standing there with my hands in my pockets, waiting, when I saw Paul all by himself squatting by the ground near the fence. I had no idea what he was doing, but I recognized him as the boy I had seen around. I also recognized him from living on my street.

I wouldn't have said anything to him except that Mother had just given me a lecture about how, if I ever saw a kid playing alone, I should play with them so they weren't lonely. She told me that if other kids saw me playing with the kid who was alone, they would want to play too and then everybody would be happy and playing together.

Well, because she had just told me all this, I felt like I should go and say hi to Paul, even though I was nervous. I walked over to him and said, "Hi."

Paul looked over his shoulder at me and said, "Hello."

I stood there for a second, feeling really awkward, and scratched the back of my leg.

Finally I looked over Paul's shoulder at what he was doing and said, "What are you doing there?"

Paul moved back so I could see. "I'm playing with helicopter seeds," he said. And so he was.

He had all these seeds in front of him, and when he picked them up and dropped them, they twirled through the air to the ground, like how a helicopter's blades spin.

"Wow," I said, "that's cool."

"It is interesting," said Paul.

"Mind if I play?" I asked.

Paul split the seeds in half so we both had ten.

"It's really fun if you take them in a handful and throw them all up at once," said Paul, "but don't squeeze them or you could squish them, and then they won't fall right. Do it like this."

Paul carefully scooped up his seeds and tossed them up. They came fluttering down so wonderfully on top of our heads and got in both of our hair, which made us laugh.

I tried to pick up mine and do the same, but of course I squeezed them too hard and broke four of them, so they just plopped down.

"I'm sorry," I said. But Paul said it was all right and gave me two more, so we both had eight.

We tossed our helicopter seeds up for a long time and got along just fine, and then the helicopter seeds got boring.

"What shall we play now?" I asked.

"We could blow on dandelion seeds and make wishes," said Paul.

"Yes," I said, "let's."

We charged around the grassy field next to the swings, picking dandelions we saw and blowing on them and then screaming out what we wished for.

"I wish for a billion dollars," I said.

"I wish for a trillion dollars," Paul said.

"That's not as many as a billion," I said.

"Yes it is," Paul said.

"Nuh-uh," I said.

"I wish for a spaceship," Paul said.

"I wish for my own bottle of perfume," I said.

"I wish for a puppy," Paul said.

"I wish for two puppies," I said.

"I wish for two puppies and a kitten," Paul said.

We kept wishing for things until we were just beat, and our hair was full of dandelion seeds. When we couldn't run anymore, we plopped down on the side of the little hill next to the gym.

"What now?" wondered Paul

"Let's play family," I suggested.

I had played family a few times with some girlfriends I had, but they never played it how I wanted, and nobody ever wanted to play the part of the boy, and they usually made me do it.

"How do you play family?" asked Paul.

"It's easy," I said. "You just pretend to be a grown-up father and mother."

"Do you think we'll really become grown-ups?" asked Paul.

"I hope so," I said. "Being a kid is the worst, because you have to go to school all the time."

"Yeah," said Paul. "I'd love to be an adult and just sit around all day."

"That's what makes playing family so much fun," I said. "You can pretend to do that and nobody can stop you."

"All right," said Paul. "I'm game. Let's play it. What should I do?"

"You should come home from work," I told him, sitting up on the grass hill and starting to pull out the grass in clumps, "I'll be home cooking dinner."

"All right."

Paul stood up and walked away, then walked back and said, "Dear, I am home."

"How was your day?" I asked, pulling up the grass.

"What should I say now?" Paul whispered at me.

"Just make something up," I whispered back.

"I had a fine day," said Paul, "I sat at my desk and read the newspaper, then I read two books about sword fighting, then on the way home I pulled a poor boy's tooth out for him."

"Wow," I said. "Well, here's your dinner."

I threw the grass I had picked at Paul, and he laughed and threw some grass back. We got into a bit of a grass fight, and by the end there was grass in both of our hair.

After that was when I finally said, "What is your name, anyway?"

"I'm Paul," said Paul.

"Really?" I asked.

"Yes," he said.

"You're not lying or anything?"

"No."

The reason I was so surprised is because my father is named Paul too.

"Well, do you know my name?" I asked.

"I don't think so," said Paul.

"Do you want to know it?" I asked.

"All right," said Paul.

"But promise you won't laugh," I said.

"I promise," said Paul.

I took a deep breath and said, "My name is Maggie, but I hate it. Isn't it just the worst name you can think of?"

Paul thought for a couple of seconds with his hands on his chin. "I can think of a worse name," he said.

"What is it?" I asked.

"Boogerface."

When I heard that I really did laugh, and I laughed really loudly the way I could. It made Paul smile at his joke because I laughed that hard.

"If there was a kid called Boogerface," I said after I had laughed, "I would flick a booger right at him."

***

Now that I've thought about it, I don't think that would be a very funny thing to do at all. At the time I thought it was a scream. One thing my mother always told me about was the Golden Rule. "Do unto others as you would have them do unto you." Mother would tell me this whenever I talked about doing anything mean. That would stop me from thinking about being mean.

I would hate to have a booger flicked at me.

These days I wish someone named Boogerface would come and visit me. If someone named Boogerface appeared in front of me this instant, I would run up and hug them and say, "I'm so thankful that you are alive."

***

Well, Paul and I tried to think of other funny names, and we really did our best.

When recess was almost over, I said to Paul, "Should we play together again at recess tomorrow?"

Paul agreed to it, and that is what we did.

The next day at recess I told Paul that we lived on the same street.

"We do?" he said.

"Yes," I said, "and I'd just love it if you came over sometime. We could play in my backyard, which is just a tops backyard. I've got a really great treehouse with a slide and a ladder on it."

"I'm not really allowed to leave my own yard," said Paul.

"That's all right," I said, after thinking. "I can just come over to your house, and we can play there. How is your backyard, though?"

"It's all right. It's got a good spot to fly a kite when the wind is just right, because there are no trees in that direction. There's also a grill, but I'm not allowed to touch it."

"I'm probably not allowed to touch it either, then," I said. "But that's all right, anyway. I don't know a thing about grilling. It would be nice to play pretend grilling though, wouldn't it? We could make grass burgers."

"If we got grass on Father's grill he'd be really upset," said Paul.

"Well, I know that," I said. "I was only saying, what if."

\*\*\*

I went to Paul's house for the first time that Saturday. I just walked there because I didn't have a bike yet. When I got there, Paul was playing in the driveway with a red wagon. I offered to give him a ride.

"Yoooo!" said Paul, as we went around in circles in his driveway. We played with that wagon all day long that day.

Isn't that a great way to meet someone? I think everyone should meet each other like that.

\*\*\*

My favorite memory of Paul is from one time when we were in Paul's backyard playing catch with a baseball he had. I tried to catch a high throw and tumbled back into a rosebush that Paul's mother had planted. I cut my arm on a thorn.

My arm started to bleed where I got cut, and Paul ran up to me. It was the most worried I had ever seen him. "Are you all right, Maggie?" he said, looking at every inch of me all at once, to make sure I wasn't hurt.

When he saw my arm, he nearly fainted. "Oh my goodness," he said, and he just grabbed my arm without even thinking, it seemed like. It did hurt, but it wasn't that bad. I was crying, but only a little. I was trying to stop crying so Paul wouldn't worry so much.

"It'll be all right," said Paul, holding my arm, even though he was getting my blood on his hand. "It'll be all right. I'm so sorry about this. It's all my fault, completely. I'm really just completely sorry to you, Maggie. If you forgive me, I'll run across the country and back. Are you all right? Oh, I'm such a mess. I've got to be more careful. Please don't blame me, Maggie."

"I'm all right, I'm all right," I said as quickly as possible, to shut Paul up. He was just going on and on.

Paul ran inside and brought out his mother and a first aid kit. Paul's mother wiped the blood away with a cotton ball and this liquid stuff. It burned the cut so bad that I couldn't understand how it was supposed to fix anything. After she had cleaned the blood off, she put a Band-Aid on my arm and left me and Paul be.

Paul was looking at my bandaged arm with this really worried face, so I stuck my arm out and said, "Look at it, Paul. It's just fine."

What happened next shocked me so much that I was practically swept off my feet.

Paul leaned forward when my arm was out and kissed it right on the spot where the Band-Aid was. All the pain went away immediately. It felt as if Paul had sucked out the pain with his lips. It was a miracle.

Paul blushed after he kissed me, and he said, "So what. You're supposed to kiss injuries. It fixes them right away."

\*\*\*

Maybe the reason everybody died of the Durmon virus is because people weren't kissing each other's hearts to fix them right away. Maybe Paul's kiss that day is what made me immune.

\*\*\*

All that I really know is that, nothing has ever felt as good as Paul kissing my arm to fix it right away felt.

I love that memory because it is a memory of Paul caring for me. It was so nice to feel as if Paul cared for me. It was nice to feel as if Paul was worried about me. It was nice to play catch with Paul too. It was just nice to be with

Paul. Paul was the pleasantest and the nicest and the best boy I knew. He didn't laugh at fart jokes, and he didn't ever say I had cooties because I was a girl. He was always brave, even though he wasn't very tall.

\*\*\*

I did get picked on at school from time to time because I was a bit different from everybody else; I was loud and silly and dumb sometimes, and my lunchbox was a paper sack instead of a tin box with a handle on it, and things like that. The boys could be mean to me, especially. Sometimes, the tall boys would stand around me and call me "Haggie" until I just wanted to cry.

When the boys did this to me and Paul heard it, he just got so angry that he marched right up between the boys and me. He was breathing really heavily and his chest was puffed up, so he looked three times his size. He stood with his hands as fists, and he said, "If you don't leave her alone, I'll sock your jaw, and I don't even care."

The biggest boy pushed Paul into me, and I caught him and held him up. Paul pushed the biggest boy, and the biggest boy hardly moved. Instead, the biggest boy shoved Paul to the ground. When Paul hit the ground, it knocked the wind out of him. I could tell because he held his stomach and moaned softly.

This made me so mad and angry that I charged at the biggest boy, and I actually did knock him down. I tugged on his hair and tweaked his nose until he was just screaming like the littlest baby.

I got into trouble for that, and Paul got in trouble too, and so did the biggest boy.

That day I learned that no matter how bothered you get by somebody, if you get violent back at them, then you're not all that great yourself. But it's so hard to not fight back when you're in a spot like that. You want to fight back more than anything. It's important to try not to fight every chance you get. When you fight, you just get yourself hurt and hurt other people, which isn't very good, and doesn't help anybody.

You can only fight when it's really necessary.

Mother told me that the only time I should fight was if someone else's life was in danger, or if my own life was in danger, or if a grownup was trying to take me away or do something wrong or nasty with me. She told me that there are times to fight, and other times when the best thing to do is to tell a teacher or a mother what is going on, so that they can handle it. It's fine by me. I don't really want to fight too much. I only pushed the biggest kid because of what he did to Paul, anyway.

Mother said the reason the biggest boy was bothering me was because he was actually very sad, and so pushing him and hurting him only made him feel worse, and what he needed was to feel better.

***

Kissing a wound is the quickest way to fix it right away.

***

That day when Paul stood between me and the biggest boy was when I saw how brave he really was. The bravest thing you can do is stand up in front of something that you know you can't beat and say, "I know I'm going to lose, but I've got to fight anyway."

***

You've really got to be very brave in order to live, don't you? All that life is, is just a big thing that stands in front of you that you know you can't beat.

***

"I know I'm going to lose, but I've got to fight anyway."

***

And that's how I met Paul.

# Chapter 28

That is pretty much everything that has happened.

*** 

I don't stay at Paul's house anymore, or any house on my old street for that matter, because I emptied them all of food. I'm on a new street now, in a nice blue house with loads of cans of food in the basement. Whoever lived here had the good sense to be prepared.

I think I must be immune to the Durmon virus. I wonder every day if I'm going to die, and every day I don't die. I just keep living. I don't really care if I have the virus or not, to be honest. Someday, maybe tomorrow, maybe in a million years, I'm going to die. If all I do is worry about dying then I'll never be able to get anything done.

*** 

I used to be so afraid of dying. I was afraid the house would catch fire, or I would get shot, or I would fall into quicksand, or a car would hit me, or I would drown in a pool, or I would get sick.

I'm not afraid of that anymore.

***

The thing to remember when you get afraid of dying is that you're not actually dying. You're still alive. You're just afraid is all. It's fine to be afraid of dying, you just have to remember that you're still alive, after.

Being afraid of dying is really no different from being afraid of spiders or snakes. Just don't think about them. If you do think about them, remember that there are happy things to think about too, like birds and songs.

***

And another thing: For goodness sake, if you can be with people, do it. Don't spend all your time alone. Being alone is the worst thing I have ever had to do.

***

I think about Paul often, and about Mother, and about Paula. I'm sure I'll see them all again. I'm sure Paul will come waltzing back to his house in a year or so with an eye patch or something, feeling fit as a fiddle. I'm sure mother will come back too, and she'll be with Father, and the two of them will have a new baby, which will be a baby brother for me to play with. I'm sure that baby will be named something just awful like Hank or Don. My parents are so bad at picking names.

When I see Paul, even though he only has one eye, I'm going to run up to him and hug him and squeeze him so tight that his other eye pops right out. I don't care if it makes him blind, I'm going to do it. Just you watch.

"Paul," I'll say to him. "It's about time you showed up."

"Maggie," he'll say, "I've missed you more than anything, even more than the eye I lost."

"However did you lose it?" I'll ask.

"Well," he'll say, "as I was hiking home to see you again, I was attacked by a pack of wolves. I fought them off with my bare hands. Thinking of seeing you gave me the strength to do it. One of them scratched my eye out in the battle, but I still managed to win. I beat the wolves so much that they ran away and vowed never to attack me again."

"How brave," I'll say.

"That was nothing," he'll say. "You should have seen me scale mountains, swing from vines, and run through a herd of raging buffalo just to get to you."

"Oh, Paul," I'll say.

It'll be like a scene from one of those romantic movies. We'll be all grown-up. I'll be tall and gorgeous with a big afro, and Paul will be handsome, with large muscles, and his hair combed just perfectly. He'll even be dressed in a navy uniform.

We'll kiss each other right there out in the street, and Mother, Father, and baby Hank or Don will cheer. It'll be the grandest reunion of all time.

But of course, before any of that can happen, I'll have to grow up, and get tall and gorgeous.

Right now I'm planning on taking a trip to the desert where Paula lives. I'm pretty sure she's still alive. She was my last living friend, and so I've got to check and see. After all, it wasn't as if she stopped sending me letters, it was just that the mailman stopped coming by.

Yes, I'm certain she's still alive too. I wouldn't be surprised if she's just as immune to the virus as I am. Anyway, there's only one way to find out.

I've found a map, and I've found her address on it. I've drawn a line from her address to mine, so I know exactly where to go.

I'll be taking my pink bike and my pop gun with me.

\*\*\*

This is what I'm doing, if you're wondering where I am. I am going off to find Paula.

\*\*\*

I'm not scared of anything, because I know everything's going to be all right in the end. I've packed lots of food, I've packed *The Orphanage on Palmer Street*, I've packed a canteen full of water, and I've packed some great skipping rocks just in case I come across a lake or something.

After I find Paula, who knows, maybe I'll swim down to the bottom of the ocean to see what's there…

\*\*\*

If you're concerned about me, I'll just say this: Don't worry about me. I'll be all right.

\*\*\*

I really will be all right.

***

One last thing: There was only one part of *The Orphanage on Palmer Street* that I didn't like. It was the way it ended. I don't mean the way the story ended, I mean the way that at the end of the book it said, "The End." I don't like it when a story ends that way. When a book ends that way, you can't tell what happens next.

I like it best when a story ends with, "And they all lived happily ever after."